THIS DIARY BELONGS TO:

Trudy Alice 'Blue' Weston

AGE: 11

ADDRESS:

Hillrose Park,

Hardbake Plains, Australia

Books by Katrina Nannestad

RED DIRT
Diaries

Katrina Nannestad

ABC
Books

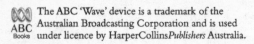
The ABC 'Wave' device is a trademark of the Australian Broadcasting Corporation and is used under licence by HarperCollins*Publishers* Australia.

First published in Australia in 2010
This edition published in 2014
by HarperCollins*Children's Books*
a division of HarperCollins*Publishers* Australia Pty Limited
ABN 36 009 913 517
harpercollins.com.au

HarperCollins*Publishers*
Level 13, 201 Elizabeth Street, Sydney NSW 2000, Australia
Unit D1, 63 Apollo Drive, Rosedale, Auckland 0632, New Zealand
A 53, Sector 57, Noida, UP, India
77–85 Fulham Palace Road, London W6 8JB, United Kingdom
2 Bloor Street East, 20th floor, Toronto, Ontario M4W 1A8, Canada
195 Broadway, New York NY 10007, USA

National Library of Australia Cataloguing-in-Publication entry:

Nannestad, Katrina, author.
    Red dirt diaries / Katrina Nannestad.
    ISBN: 978 0 7333 3394 1 (pbk.)
    Nannestad, Katrina. Red dirt diaries ; 1.
    For primary school age.
    Farm life—Juvenile fiction.
    Children's stories.
    Australian Broadcasting Corporation.
A823.4

Cover design by Hazel Lam, HarperCollins Design Studio
Cover illustrations by Katrina Nannestad; background images by
shutterstock.com
Internal design by Priscilla Nielsen
Typeset by Kirby Jones
Printed and bound in Australia by McPherson's Printing Group
The papers used by HarperCollins in the manufacture of this book are
a natural, recyclable product made from wood grown in sustainable
plantation forests. The fibre source and manufacturing processes meet
recognised international environmental standards, and carry certification.

To Bloss, Sniff and Mouse

RED DIRT
Diaries

January

Sunday, 1 January

My New Year's resolutions are:

1. I will write in my diary every day.
2. I will not stress about going to boarding school next year.
3. I will *not* let Wes and Fez annoy me. (The yabby I found in my cornflakes this morning has already tested me on this one!)
4. I will pray for rain every day until the drought breaks.

No-one else in the family would write down their resolutions — probably scared they won't be able to keep them — so I am writing them here.

Dad's resolutions:

1. I will not arm wrestle with Bert Hartley (Bert dislocated Dad's shoulder last night at the Hartleys' New Year's Eve party).

2. I will not curse.
3. I will take my boots off before I come into the house. (Actually, I think these might be Mum's resolutions for him.)

Mum's resolutions:

1. I will not nag Robert about cursing and wearing his boots into the house. (Dad made her say this.)
2. I will take an hour off every Friday night to have a glass of wine out on the veranda and listen to Classic FM.
3. I will pray for rain every day until the drought breaks.

Peter's resolutions:

1. I will not curse when Mum is nearby.
2. I will make sure Mum and Dad don't get any more special repair bills for my room at boarding school.
3. I will beat Dad at arm wrestling before I turn sixteen.

Sophie's resolutions:

1. I will stop eating chocolate, chocolate biscuits, chips, ice cream, cake, puddings and any other foods that give me pimples.
2. I will file and buff my fingernails every day.
3. I will not let Justine Martin-Dodsworth pierce my bellybutton — no matter how much she nags me.

Blue (Me!) Fez Wes Fluffles

Wes's resolutions:

1. I will not stuff any more ball bearings up my nose.
2. I will brush my hair at least once a week.

Fez's resolutions:

1. I will not break any bones this year.
2. I will not stuff any more ball bearings up Wes's nose.
3. I will not call Blue 'Ranga Girl'.
4. I will remember to feed the chooks ... sometimes.

Smells like it's time to sign off for today. Mum has just taken a golden syrup pudding out of the steamer and it's begging to be eaten with bucket loads of cream and custard.

Monday, 2 January

Sophie's driving me mad. It must be something to do with turning fourteen last week and her new ambition to become a fashion designer. She's all gushy and girly and has started reading women's magazines!!!

We were trying to watch the cricket on TV this afternoon, but she kept on tugging at my arm and saying the dumbest things.

'Oh, Bluuuue! Just look at the fabric this dress is made of! It's simply gorgeous!'

Wes stuck his finger down his throat behind her back.

'I'll *die* if Mum doesn't buy herself some new clothes this year,' Sophie moaned as she shoved a magazine in my face. 'Her white linen pants are *so* outdated. It's *such* an embarrassment. What she *really* wants is a nice little pair of Capri pants like this.'

I thought what she really wanted was a new microwave and world peace!!!

'What a fabulous hairstyle!' Sophie said, just about dribbling on the page. 'I'd commit murder to have hair like that!'

'I'll commit murder if you don't shut up,' Peter grumbled from the beanbag.

Sophie threw the magazine at him and walked off in a huff.

I felt a bit sorry for her, so later on I let her braid my hair and paint my toenails pink. It paid off because Sophie did the sheep run with me before dinner.

Only two sheep got stuck in the dam today and both are still alive.

Tuesday, 3 January

Mr Ashmore gave us three pigs this afternoon — Bacon, Sausage and Salami. They are the fattest animals in the district. Mr Ashmore said they're easy to look after because you just feed them scraps and leftovers. And when they're so fat that they're about to burst, you eat them.

The Ashmores are moving to Dubbo. They can't take the pigs with them because they'll be living in town. They haven't been able to sell their farm. As Mum says, who'd pay good money for a piece of desert? Mr Ashmore shot all his sheep last week, because no-one else wanted them and he couldn't just let them starve to death.

Bacon, Sausage and Salami don't seem to mind the change. They've made themselves at home on our veranda — right near the kitchen door. Fluffles looks a bit put out.

Wednesday, 4 January

Wesley and Finlay, the grossest seven-year-olds on earth, found two dead rats in the shed today. Thankfully, Salami knocked Wes over and ate his rat before he got to the house, but Fez managed to keep the other rat safe.

They came into the lounge room and laid the dead rat on the coffee table right next to my hot chocolate and toast. Yuck!!!

'We're gunna do something really cool with it, Blue,' said Wes.

They sat staring at the rat, scratching their heads. Fez emptied his pockets onto the table, looking for inspiration — he had a broken Life Saver, two copper fencing nails, a bird's beak (!), a pocket knife, an empty lolly container, seven *live* Christmas beetles and something brown and slimy.

All Wes had was a big rubber band and a daggy red hanky that Gran gave him for Christmas. He kept looking enviously at the slimy brown thing from Fez's pocket.

Fez spread the hanky out over the rat and Wes's eyes lit up.

'Just a sec!' he yelled and disappeared into the junk room. He came back with a pair of undies from one of Sophie's old dolls. He used Fez's pocket knife to cut a hole in the undies, so that when he put them on the dead rat, its tail could stick out. Then he tied the red hanky around the rat's neck, held the rat up in the air and ran round and round the lounge room.

'Look! Up in the sky!' yelled Wes.

'It's a bird!' cried Fez.

'No! It's a plane!' said Wes, in a girly voice.

'No! It's Super Rat!' they both yelled together.

Wes and Fez think everything they do is so funny. They laughed so hard that Wes snorted three ball bearings out of his nose that Fez had stuck up there on New Year's Eve.

This is the sort of stuff we have to put up with all the time with 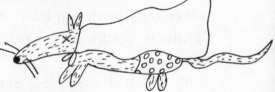 Wes and Fez, the moronic twins.

I think Dad likes the pigs.

He doesn't really take much notice of any of the animals, except when he's working. He ignores Fluffles completely, even when she rubs up against his legs, and he says the dogs are not to be patted and played with, because they're working dogs, not pets and we shouldn't spoil them.

But today I caught him scratching Bacon behind the ear and I'm pretty sure I heard him call her 'Old Girl'. It's bad enough that Wes and Fez are insane, without Dad losing it too.

Thursday, 5 January

Super Rat made a surprise appearance at lunch time. He was hiding in the pumpkin scones. Mum was furious. Dad says Wes and Fez are high-spirited, but we all know that's just a nice way of saying they're complete maniacs.

Won't be long before the dams are nothing but mud. More and more sheep are getting stuck when they go down to drink and they're so weak from hunger they can't pull themselves out again. Had to rescue four today.

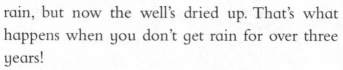

We used to pump water up from the well when we didn't get enough rain, but now the well's dried up. That's what happens when you don't get rain for over three years!

I remember it rained four Christmases ago, because the house dam overflowed and water ran straight down our hallway, taking Wes and all our Christmas presents out the front door and half a kilometre down the driveway. Thankfully, we got most of the presents back. Unfortunately, some idiot (Peter?) rescued Wes and brought him home too. But I really can't remember a decent downpour since.

Now there's not a blade of grass to be seen. The paddocks are just bare dirt and even that looks like disappearing in the dust storms. All that the poor sheep get to eat is one lousy bale of hay a day.

Makes me feel guilty about scoffing lamingtons while I write this.

Friday, 6 January

Dad gave Super Rat a serve this afternoon. Super Rat was hiding in his work boot. Dad swore (there goes his first New Year's resolution!) and threw Super Rat as far as he could.

Super Rat flew heroically through the air, until his undies got snagged on the branch of a peppercorn tree.

'Cool!' said Wes.

'Safety undies!' said Fez.

Saturday, 7 January

Sophie dyed her hair today. It's bright pink. She's hysterical because she looks like a character from the Muppets, when she wanted to look like the auburn-haired beauty on page ninety-five of her *Beautiful Woman* magazine.

That's what happens when you use red food colouring instead of hair dye.

It's not easy for Sophie, living two hours away from any decent shops.

Mum was pretty understanding about it. She said she'd take Sophie to town to get it fixed up at the hairdressers before she goes back to boarding school.

Wes and Fez were not so understanding. They rescued Super Rat from the tree, stole the rest of the red food colouring and dyed Super Rat's mangy hair bright pink.

Wes said, 'Look, Sophie! You look just like Super Rat!'

Pink People

Sophie burst into tears and ran into our bedroom, slamming the door behind her.

Fez said, 'You'd think she'd be pleased, Blue. I'd love to look as cool as Super Rat.'

Sunday, 8 January

Mum, Sophie and I pulled five sheep from the dams today. Only two were still alive. Dad also shot two sheep. They were on their sides shaking, too weak from hunger to get up. He had to put the poor things out of their misery.

Dad drove straight back to the house and renamed the pigs — Doris, Mildred and Gertrude. He said he'd be damned if he was going to let anyone eat the only three healthy beasts in the district.

Monday, 9 January

Today we discovered that the walls in Wes and Fez's bedroom have glass mixed in with the mud.

We knew there was straw, horsehair, old sheep bones, barbed wire and stones in the mud walls, because every now and then a bit of wall crumbles off, leaving stuff sticking out.

I suppose people had to make do with whatever they could find back when Great Great Grandpa Weston built the house over a hundred years ago.

When we were little, we were terrified of going to bed at night because of the bones that would crumble out of the walls.

'Mummy! Mummy! There's a dead man hanging out of the wall above my bed!'

'Daddy! Daddy! Great Uncle Tommy's toes just fell onto my pillow!'

Peter used to tell us that the bones were the remains of some poor farmhand who Great Great Grandpa Weston murdered and plastered up inside the walls. He said that the mud crumbled off when the farmhand's ghost tried to escape his mud wall prison.

I still find it a bit creepy sometimes.

Anyway, back to the good bit ... Wes and Fez were fighting over whose bed Super Rat was going to sleep in that night, and Fez pushed Wes against their bedroom wall with all his might. Wes cut his bum on a piece of glass that was poking out of the wall and had to get seven stitches. Ha, ha, ha!

Mum got Mr Sweeney, the vet, to stitch him up because the nearest doctor is nearly eighty kilometres away.

Wes was bawling his eyes out the whole time because he was terrified that Mr Sweeney was going to put him down.

If only!

Tuesday, 10 January

Woke up this morning covered in two centimetres of red dirt.

Sophie said now she knows what it feels like to be dead and buried.

We folded our quilts up carefully to carry the dirt outside, but I don't know why we bothered. The whole house was covered in dirt anyway — floors, tables, lounges, shelves. Even the pictures on the walls had dirt stuck in the little grooves of the frames. There'd been a dust storm overnight and somebody's paddock — maybe ours, maybe someone else's from a hundred kilometres away — ended up in our house. It blew in under the doors and through the cracks around the windows.

Mum was crying when Sophie and I went in to her bedroom. Dad says Mum's a toughy, but I've seen her cry a few times since the drought got really bad.

Even Wes and Fez must have realised how fed up Mum was, because Super Rat delivered a bunch of plastic flowers and tea and toast to her at about eleven o'clock.

It took us until after dark to get the house cleaned. We had a really late supper out on the veranda, but Mum didn't eat a thing. She just fiddled with a piece of toast and mumbled something about endless dust.

Dad gave Mum a long hug and said, 'Oh, well … I s'pose it could be worse.'

That's Dad's answer to anything bad.

A fire will sweep through the entire wheat crop a week before he's due to harvest, and he'll say, 'Oh, well … I s'pose it could be worse.'

Crows will peck the eyes out of half the newborn lambs, and he'll say, 'Oh, well … I s'pose it could be worse.'

If the earth opened up and swallowed the house with Mum and all us kids in it, the sheep turned into maggots and a meteorite was headed straight for him, he'd probably just shrug his shoulders and say, 'Oh, well … I s'pose it could be worse.'

Mum looked like she was going to cry again, but Doris, Mildred and Gertrude came snuffling around the corner making funny, gentle piggy noises and she began to laugh. Gertrude knocked a plate of crumpets onto the veranda and gobbled them all up.

Wednesday, 11 January

Wes and Fez got tired of Super Rat's lack of energy today, so they decided that he needed to learn to fly on his own. They nicked a fan belt from the machinery shed and used it like a slingshot to launch Super Rat from the roof. Sophie, Peter and I were all invited.

Super Rat flew through the air, his cape flapping heroically in the wind, until he splatted into the windscreen of Father O'Malley's car as he arrived for a visit.

Fez laughed so hard that he fell off the roof and split his head open.

Fez   Wes

Wes laughed so hard at Fez that he doubled over and split the stitches in his bum.

Mum had to ring Mr Sweeney to come and stitch them both up, so she said he might as well bring Mrs Sweeney and stay for dinner with Father O'Malley.

After dinner, the adults talked for hours about the drought. Father O'Malley asked Mum and Dad and the Sweeneys if they'd thought about moving off the land!!!!

Father O'Malley is a nice bloke, but that was a really dumb question.

Mr Sweeney stared at his hands for a while, then said he'd die first.

BRAVO!

Dad said that his father was born at Hillrose Park, and his grandfather before that. He said the Westons are born with red dirt between their toes.

Mum said that explained the state of the carpet in the lounge room.

Thursday, 12 January

Sophie and I opened a packet of chocolate biscuits on the back veranda today, and next thing we knew Doris and Mildred were bolting across the back yard like two greyhounds after a bunny. They must have heard the rustle of the biscuit packet. I didn't know pigs could run so fast!

Sophie's hair is fading. Now it's the colour of fairyfloss and she looks more like a pixie than a Muppet. I told her this, but she didn't seem too happy. Instead of thanking me for the compliment, she told me she was sure my nose had twice as many freckles as it did this time last year, and no wonder because it's wide enough to have a whole mural painted on it.

I thought that was a bit mean.

Friday, 13 January

Got a postcard from Mat today. She's down at the beach with her Gran and Pop, and won't be back until the end of the holidays. I think all that fresh ocean air is going to her head. This is what she wrote:

Hi Blue,

Having a fab time here — the beach is to die for!

Yesterday I went to one of those fancy little manicure salons. Now my nails are blue with teeny-weeny palm trees on them — so cute!

I've become friends with a girl in the caravan next to ours. Her name's Angelina and guess what? She'll be going to boarding school in Bathurst with us next year! Isn't that exciting?

Love,
Mat

Yuck!

There's absolutely nothing exciting about boarding school.

Just because our school only goes to year six, everyone thinks they have to send their kids away for high school. It's horrible.

Haven't they heard of correspondence school? Or hiring a governess?

I never want to leave home. I'm sure I was born with some of that red dirt between my toes.

If I get sent to boarding school, I'm going to run away, like Judy in *Seven Little Australians*.

She runs away and walks for miles and miles until she makes it back home. Her dad gets really mad, but then she gets a disease called tuberculosis, so he forgives her and lets her stay. They all live happily ever after.

Well, almost. She gets killed by a falling tree in the end.

I want to be just like Judy.

Saturday, 14 January

Peter opened a packet of chips near the back door today and Doris and Mildred came sprinting across the yard. They pressed their snouts against the screen door and snorted and drooled.

Wes and Fez thought it was so funny that they grabbed a can of baked beans, walked about 300 metres down the driveway and started opening it. Sure enough, Doris and Mildred came running around the side of the house and galloped down the driveway towards the baked beans.

Wes and Fez had a great day getting the pigs to run from one end of the farm to the other just by shaking a box of cereal, scraping a fork across a plate, opening a jar of jam or cracking a walnut. Doris and Mildred are so greedy.

Gertrude is greedy too, but she's too lazy to run after food. She just lies at the back door, waiting for someone to throw her some scraps from the kitchen. She even tries to eat Fluffles' cat food, but Fluffles hisses and scratches until Gerty gives up.

Sunday, 15 January

Drove into Hardbake Plains for the monthly church service this morning. Went to put my good sandals on and they wouldn't fit. My toes were hanging over the end by miles. I must have the biggest feet of any eleven-year-old this side of the black stump.

Gabby Woodhouse was dead jealous of Sophie's pink hair. Gabby's mad on hairdressing. She spent the whole church service trying to colour her hair pink with her little sister's new felt-tip pens instead of listening to Father O'Malley and praying for the drought to end.

Wes and Fez spent the whole church service drawing billycarts on the back page of their hymn book. Mum'll kill them if she finds out.

Four sheep rescued from the dams today and all still alive. Hooray!

Monday, 16 January

Doris and Mildred have bionic hearing! Sophie 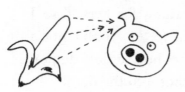 peeled a banana near the clothesline this morning and Doris and Mildred appeared from nowhere before she took the first bite. HOW MUCH NOISE DOES PEELING A BANANA MAKE?!?

We got rain today. It clouded over, sprinkled for about ten seconds, the sky cleared and that was the end of that.

Tuesday, 17 January

44°C today.

I feel *so* dehydrated.

Can people turn to dust?

Wednesday, 18 January

Mum took me and Sophie over to Dubbo today.

Sophie has blonde hair again. It looks a little bit dull now that we're all used to it being pink.

She wanted the hairdresser to dye it auburn, but Mum said it would look trashy. Like pink hair didn't!!!

I got new sandals for my giant feet, a book and a pair of shorts. I wanted three books, but Mum didn't buy a single thing for herself, so I didn't think it would be fair to ask. Sophie got a pink bikini. Won't the leeches have a field day on her belly when she wears that into the dam!

We ran into Mrs Ashmore in town. She said she's going to start working at a solicitor's office next week and won't it be a novelty to have money in her purse? She seemed *glad* to be gone from Hardbake Plains!!! Some people don't make any sense at all. She said Mr Ashmore misses the farm. Well, DUH!

Mum took us to a café for lunch and to the movies. Afterwards, she said we couldn't really afford it but there had to be some fun in the middle of this bleeding drought.

I cried all the way home.

Thursday, 19 January

Got a whopper dust storm today. We couldn't play outside and Mum was stomping around the house like a mad woman, plugging newspapers and bits of foil into the gaps around the doors and windows, so we went into the chicken coop to play Truth or Dare.

Sophie dared Fez to kiss Esmeralda on the head. Esmeralda is sitting on her eggs at the moment and has totally lost her sense of humour. Fez got a bloody nose, because Es managed to get her beak right up his nostril and took a chunk out of him.

Wes chose Truth and had to tell us the dumbest thing he'd ever done. It must have been hard for him to decide, because there were just so many things to choose from. Finally he settled on peeing on the electric fence — a SHOCKING experience!

Peter chose Truth too, and had to tell us the naughtiest thing he'd ever done at boarding school. He said it was accidentally setting fire to the dormitory curtains, when he and his mates were lighting their farts in the dark.

Wes and Fez cheered. Sophie tried to look disgusted, but burst out laughing.

Then Peter started to tell us about the time he and his friend Xiu put laxatives in the chocolate custard while the kitchen ladies were having a tea break. I told him to shut up. You're only meant to give one Truth, not a whole speech. Anyway, I hate it when Sophie and Peter talk about boarding school, especially if it sounds as though they have fun there. How could they possibly like being away from Mum and Dad and the farm?

Wes and Fez were mad at me for stopping Peter's story, so they dared me to sit out on the veranda until the dust storm was over. I was really mad at Peter and wanted to get away, so I did it. The others went inside the house to watch TV.

It was dreadful. I could barely breathe and I had to keep my eyes clamped shut. By the time the storm had passed, my hair was stiff with dust and my feet were buried in topsoil. When I blew my nose, mud came out!!!

All Mum's washing had blown over to the shearing shed, where it was half-buried. Sophie's blue-and-white banana bed hung off the top of the tank, and dirt was banked up against the trees and fence posts. A mob of dusty, skinny ewes wobbled past, bleating stupidly. They weren't meant to be anywhere near the house.

I called out to Dad and he and Peter came out onto the veranda, pulling on their boots. We jumped in the ute and drove off to check the fences.

Dad sure swore *a lot* when we found the

problem — not a hole or broken piece of wire in sight. The wind had blown dry tumbleweed up against the fence, then blown dust and dirt against the tumbleweed until huge mounds had formed. The sheep had walked up and over the fence on a ramp made out of paddock soil!!!

Don't know why they bothered really. The grass is hardly greener on the other side of the fence.

Friday, 20 January

This afternoon Sophie covered our bedroom walls with pictures of supermodels and daft blokes. She said they were not daft blokes. They were hunky movie stars and rock singers. I tore the pictures off the wall on my side of the room and stuck up pictures of harvesters, stud bulls and wheat crops from Dad's calendar and told her to get a grip on herself. We lived on a farm, not in Hollywood, and who the heck did she think she was anyway?

Mum came in and sided with Sophie. CAN YOU BELIEVE IT?!?

Mum said that the farm was not everything … that there were indeed other people, places and experiences out there in the world for us to enjoy … that Sophie was just taking an interest in normal things … that this was why it was so important for us to go to boarding school, so we could experience things beyond country life … so we could make healthy choices for our lives …

AAARRGGHH!!!

My own mother, a traitor!

I've started reading *Seven Little Australians* again. I read the first three chapters out loud to Gertrude and she seemed to be quite absorbed in it. Then again, it could have been the ginger-nut biscuits I was sharing with her that kept her interested.

Saturday, 21 January

Wes and Fez have pulled their bicycles apart and are making two billycarts. Don't know how they'll pick up any speed with them because there are no hills around here.

Sophie and I pulled three sheep out of the muddy dams today and then I got stuck! Sophie waded back in to pull me out and she got stuck too! You'd think the sheep would do something to help after all the times we've rescued them, but the stupid things just stood there and stared at us.

We had to wait nearly an hour before Mum realised we were missing. She and Dad rode over on the motorbike and pulled us out.

When I took my gumboots off at home, my feet were covered in leeches.

'Cool,' said Wes.

'Leech Girl!' said Fez.

If anyone else called me Leech Girl I'd deck them, but with Wes and Fez that sort of thing is a compliment.

I'm halfway through *Seven Little Australians*.

Sunday, 22 January

Helped Dad repaint the sign at our front gate today. He said he was sick to death of shooting sheep and watching things fall apart around here. Today was his day to make something better.

We started by painting the background of the sign a lovely creamy colour, and while that was drying we sat under the peppercorn tree and drank tea and ate ham and relish sandwiches.

My very first memory is of a picnic with Dad. We were in the shearing shed, and Dad sat me up on a bale of wool. I can still remember my little yellow gumboots, the sickly sweet smell of the wool, and the taste of devon sandwiches.

Dad and I got to wondering how the farm got its name. I mean, Hillrose Park is a really dumb name. For starters, there isn't a hill for hundreds of miles around. Everything is dead flat. There aren't any roses either. We've got geraniums, tumbleweed, thistles and catheads, but no roses.

Dad said that the Park bit actually makes sense, because we do *park* the car in the carport, we *park* the tractor and the harvester in the machine shed and we *park* our backsides at the kitchen table each morning for cereal, sausages and eggs.

Even so, Hillrose Park is not the most sensible name for our farm. I thought we should rename the property Geranium Run or Cathead Flats, but Dad said Hillrose Park was probably the name of Great Great Grandpa Weston's home in England and we'd better honour tradition.

I got three quarters of the way through painting the letters on the sign, when Super Rat came flying through the air and knocked the paint tin off the top of the sign. It bounced off my hand and made me drop my paintbrush in the dirt.

I thought Super Rat was destroyed when he flew into Father O'Malley's windscreen, but apparently he wasn't. I can tell you now, though, that he is well and truly out of action! Dad saw to that.

We don't have any more brown paint for the letters, so now the sign at our front gate says Hillrose Po (I didn't even get to put the stick on the 'a'!) with a blob running down below the 'o'.

Monday, 23 January

Wes and Fez found some black paint and finished the sign at the front gate. They added an extra 'o' and painted an arrow, so now the sign says Hillrose Poo with an arrow pointing to the brown blob of paint, which really does look like a poo.

They are still working on their billycarts and torturing Doris and Mildred, luring them all over the farm by shaking cereal boxes and rustling food wrappers. They said it's fitness training. Fitness training for what?

You'd think with all that running Doris and Mildred would slim down a bit, but they seem to get fatter every day. I think Dad's been sneaking them treats from the pantry. Meanwhile, the sheep and Mum seem to get skinnier every day. I'm sure the only thing holding the sheep's bones together is their fleece. I don't know what's holding Mum together ...

Got another postcard from Mat. She said she has kissed a boy on the jetty! She could have done the normal thing and kissed him on the lips. Ha! Ha! Ha!

I was about to tear the postcard up in disgust, but decided to give it to Sophie. I said that she should go live at the Sweeneys' place. She and Mat could talk about boys and leave me in peace.

Tuesday, 24 January

Finished reading *Seven Little Australians*. I cried when Judy died. She was so good to save her baby brother. If Wes or Fez were standing under a falling tree, there's no way I'd risk my life to save them. In fact, I don't think I'd even bother to yell, 'Look out!'

Wednesday, 25 January

It all makes sense now. Well, as much sense as anything Wes and Fez do could possibly make.

The twin tornadoes have been making *pig chariots*, not billycarts. They have rope harnesses for the pigs and little sticks with chocolate bickies dangling off them that they hover just in front of the pigs' snouts. The driveway is the racetrack — three kilometres to the front gate and the Hillrose Poo sign.

They had their first races today. Wes raced with Doris. Fez raced with Mildred. Peter stood at the front gate with the finishing flag — a pair of Dad's boxer shorts tied to a broom handle. Sophie blew an old plastic recorder as the starting signal. I sat on the tractor wreck halfway between the house and the Hillrose Poo sign and laughed my head off.

It's amazing how fast those pigs will run if you dangle a piece of food in front of them.

It's also incredible how high into the air a pig chariot flies when it hits a rock at top speed. Fez broke his collarbone, got two black eyes and grazed half his face off. He also won the first four races before he crashed, so he was pretty pleased.

Mr Sweeney said Fez should keep his arm in a sling and lay off pig racing for a few weeks until his collarbone mended.

Wes is really jealous of Fez's black eyes. He's been begging Peter to punch him in the eye all night. I offered to do it, but Mum wouldn't let me.

Thursday, 26 January, Australia Day
Dad and Peter shot thirteen sheep today.

They didn't say a word at dinner time. They didn't notice all the little Australian flags we had stuck in the mashed potato.

Dad didn't even say, 'Oh, well ... I s'pose it could be worse.'

Friday, 27 January
I've taught Gertrude to carry the peg bucket to the clothesline! It took a loaf of bread, four crumpets and a whole chocolate cake to encourage her, but it was worth it in the end.

Mum was upset about the chocolate cake. We were going to the Sweeneys' in the afternoon to play tennis, and she'd just baked it to take with us.

It was a bit boring at the Sweeneys' house without Mat and Lynette there, but their cat had just had kittens, so Sophie and I played with them for a while. We also beat Mum and Mrs Sweeney six–one at tennis. We would have beaten them six–love, but I tripped over my big feet at a crucial moment.

Saturday, 28 January

Raced Wes in the pig chariots. Wes and Doris won because I was scared and kept pulling on the reins to slow Mildred down.

Peter was about to challenge Wes, but Doris gobbled up the chocolate biscuit on Mildred's stick before the race began and Mildred got nasty. She reared up, throwing Peter out of the chariot, then turned around and bit his ear. Peter rolled around on the ground half-laughing, half-moaning with pain.

Fez gave Mildred a bag of chips as a reward.

Sunday, 29 January

Mum taught me how to make steamed golden syrup pudding today. I was so proud of it. It looked perfect and smelled delicious as I carried it from the kitchen into the dining room.

Gertrude must have thought it smelled delicious too, because she tore through the flyscreen on the back door, bolted into the dining room and knocked me over. The pudding splattered onto the floor and Gertrude gobbled up every last blob of it.

At least we still had custard.

Monday, 30 January

Sophie, Peter, Fluffles and I went rat hunting in the hayshed this morning. Peter made me this great new slingshot. Didn't get any rats, but we saw a very big brown snake. Dad always says the snakes are more scared of us than we are of them. All I can say is that there must be one extremely terrified snake out there this afternoon.

Mat comes home on Friday. Can't wait to see her. She is my best friend after all, and maybe she will go back to normal when she gets back home among decent country folk.

Kissing a boy on the jetty. How could she? YUCK!!!

Tuesday, 31 January

Wes and Fez have dug a hole right through their bedroom wall. I think they were looking for the murdered farmhand's skeleton. They got carried away and took to the wall with Dad's spade drill, and next thing they knew, sunlight was shining in through a hole in the mud wall. The hole is just big enough for Gerty to stick her snout through and beg for food.

Mum was furious and told them to go outside and race their pig chariots.

Don't suppose she cares about Fez's broken collarbone as much as she cares about the house. Then again, if she lets Wes and Fez continue their search for skeletons, they may do away with whole walls and then the house will collapse and we'll all be squished to death. It *is* better that she sacrifice Fez for the sake of the rest of us!

All the poor suckers in the other half of the state go back to school tomorrow. Here, out west, we may have drought, mouse plagues, heat waves, dust storms and Wes and Fez, but we get an extra week's summer holiday. Hooray!

february

Wednesday, 1 february

The new school teacher is here, in my bed, sleeping. I'm not sure whether it's because of the painkillers Mr Sweeney gave her, or if she's unconscious again.

She's really pretty with pale, peachy skin and long, curly hair the colour of carrots. But what I like best about her is her nose. It's wide and covered in freckles! I just know we'll be kindred spirits with our matching carrot-tops and noses … if only she can forgive us!

It's all thanks to Wes and Fez, of course. Well, Wes and Fez *and* the pigs *and* the drought *and* the dust, if you want to get technical.

Miss McKenzie was on her way to Hardbake Plains to find somewhere to live before school starts next week. She's going to be the new teacher. Up until now we've only had Mr Cluff, but the school has become disadvantaged. I thought it was because of Wes and Fez, but it's something to do with all the parents being so poor because of the drought. Apparently it's an advantage to be disadvantaged, because they said we can now have a second teacher, even though there are only nineteen children in the school. Well, seventeen, plus Wes and Fez, who are more like wild animals than children.

Anyway, Miss McKenzie was driving to the Bake this afternoon. A dust storm was brewing and she couldn't see the road properly, so she pulled into our driveway and parked inside the front gate near the Hillrose Poo sign. She unwrapped a block of chocolate, snapped off a row, and started to eat it.

Meanwhile, Wes and Fez were racing towards the front gate in their pig chariots. They couldn't see for more than a metre in front of them because of the dust storm. Mildred and Doris couldn't see through the dust either, but Wes reckons they must have heard the sound of FOOD with their bionic piggy hearing. The wind was howling, the chariots were rumbling, Wes and Fez were yelling and Miss McKenzie was inside her car with the windows wound up, but Wes swears those greedy sows could still hear the snap of a row of chocolate being broken off!

Doris lurched forward, throwing Wes out of his chariot, and bolted towards the front gate. Mildred also sped up and veered to the side of the road where Doris was galloping.

Unfortunately, just at that moment, a sparrow, blinded by the dust, flew straight into the driver's window of Miss McKenzie's car and fell to the ground. Miss McKenzie got out to rescue the sparrow and stood stroking its limp little body in her hands. She could barely see her shoes through the dust, let alone the approaching danger.

The pigs continued to gallop towards Miss McKenzie until, just metres in front of her, they crunched together in a high-speed collision. Fez was hurtled along the ground until he crashed into a fencepost. Doris and Mildred fell together in a groaning pile of pork. One of the chariots rolled on alone past the gate. The other chariot splintered into tiny pieces, and one of its wheels flew through the air until it hit Miss McKenzie's face, breaking her nose and knocking her unconscious.

And that's why she is now asleep in my bed.

Thursday, 2 February

Miss McKenzie is every bit as lovely as I hoped she would be. She comes from Scotland and speaks with a really cool accent — a 'lilt', Mum calls it. She has sparkly blue eyes with wrinkles around them. I'm sure the wrinkles are from smiling so much, because she is only twenty-six. She also has a bit of bruising around her eyes, but Mr Sweeney said this will fade over the next few days.

Miss McKenzie has been thanking us all day for being so friendly. Yesterday, Mr Sweeney arrived with his vet's bag as soon as he heard that the new teacher was unconscious at our front gate, and he has been back again twice today. The second time he brought a sponge cake from Mrs Sweeney.

Mum and Dad have insisted that Miss McKenzie stay here for a few days, until she can walk without getting dizzy. Mum brewed a pot of chicken soup and made up the guest bed in the sleep-out. Dad has wiped the dust off her car and given it a grease and oil change. People in the country are really friendly, but in this case I think we all feel we owe her one (or two or three or four!).

I helped out by reading *Seven Little Australians* to Miss McKenzie while she rested.

Wes and Fez haven't dared show their faces all day. They're scared of Miss McKenzie and so they should be after what they've done.

Friday, 3 February

Miss McKenzie got out of bed after breakfast and had a cup of tea on the veranda with Mum, Sophie and me.

Gertrude knocked the plate off the table and ate the last four slices of Mrs Sweeney's sponge cake. Miss McKenzie laughed so hard that her nose began to throb and she had to go back to bed.

Wes and Fez were spying through the hole in their bedroom wall. They reckon Miss McKenzie mightn't be too scary after all.

Earlier this evening I took Miss McKenzie a mug of tea in bed. She asked why everyone called me Blue when Trudy is such a pretty name. I explained how Australians love to give people nicknames that are a bit dumb. Our Uncle Joe's as skinny as a rake but we call him Chubs. Aunty June, his wife, is tall and built like a tank so everyone calls her Flea. The bloke who owns the Hardbake Pub is always full of doom and gloom, so he's called Sunshine. I don't think anyone can even remember his real name anymore. He's just Sunshine. And then there's me. I've got red hair, so people call me Blue.

Miss McKenzie laughed and said that if they did that in Scotland, more than half her family would be called Blue.

I told her all about Hardbake Plains Public School and the kids that go there. I hinted that Mr Cluff needed a wife. She seemed to really appreciate everything and she smiled a lot.

Mat rang tonight and told me all about her holiday at the beach. She started to describe that kiss on the jetty, but I pretended to have a cake crumb stuck in my throat and coughed and coughed and hung up. I think by Wednesday she'll be back to normal.

Saturday, 4 February

Miss McKenzie collected the eggs and went on the sheep rescue run with Sophie and me today. She said her nose has stopped throbbing. I am disappointed because the swelling has gone down a bit and her nose is no longer as wide as mine.

Wes and Fez finally had to face Miss McKenzie at dinner time. They needn't have been so worried.

She said they were delightful lively lads, just like her little brother, Dougal. She told them a story about Dougal jumping off the roof of their two-storey house with only an umbrella for a parachute, and was about to tell them about an incident with a fox and a packet of chicken-flavoured biscuits, when Mum said she was sorry to interrupt (BIG LIE), but it was time for Wes and Fez to do the dishes. We all breathed a sigh of relief. Wes and Fez get into enough trouble as it is without Miss McKenzie giving them new ideas.

Before Miss McKenzie went to bed, she made Wes and Fez promise to take her for a spin in one of the pig chariots some time soon.

When she left the room, Dad said, 'She's a real good sport, that one.'

Wes said, 'Hey, Dad, can we have the wheels off your bicycle?'

Fez said, 'It's for a present for Miss McKenzie.'

Good grief! I hope she has health insurance.

Sunday, 5 February

Miss McKenzie is going to stay at Hillrose Poo!

There's absolutely nowhere for her to live at Hardbake Plains and I think Mum and Dad feel like we need to take care of her, after all that's

42

happened. I suppose if we really wanted to take care of her, we would send her far, far away from Wes and Fez, where she'd be out of harm's way, but Mum and Dad are doing the best they can.

Dad took her over to the old shearers' cottage. It was a bit grotty and had baby mice in the kitchen cupboard, but Miss McKenzie loved it.

She said, 'Och! Isn't it just grand? Just like my granny's house back in Scotland.'

I thought that was a bit weird. Our granny has peppermints and boiled lollies in her kitchen cupboard, not baby mice. But Miss McKenzie was happy and she is going to stay, so that is the main thing.

Anyway, Gertrude cleaned up the baby mice. She wandered into the kitchen, stuck her big fat head in the cupboard and gobbled them all up. Maybe she thought they were jellybeans. Pigs can be so gross.

Mum, Sophie and I spent all day helping Miss McKenzie scrub and clean the cottage from top to bottom. Mum got some extra bits and pieces from the shed, like a rocking chair and an old dresser, to make it all homely. Sophie designed and sewed some curtains out of Mum's best sheets. Mum was a bit annoyed, but Miss McKenzie thought they were beautiful, even if they were lopsided.

We even dug a little garden in front of the veranda and planted some geranium cuttings, which Miss McKenzie can water with her tea dregs and dirty dishwater. It really does look quite pretty now we're finished.

Dad made a sign to hang next to the front door. It says *Serenity Cottage*.

Miss McKenzie read the sign and said, 'Och! Isn't that sweet?'

Wes said, 'What's serenity?'

Mum looked at Wes and Fez and the plastic bag full of rubber bands, springs and dead mice they had been collecting. 'I have no idea,' she said, and went for a little lie down on her bed.

Monday, 6 February
I HATE BOARDING SCHOOL.

We have been so busy with Miss McKenzie moving in, that I forgot that Sophie and Peter would be leaving tomorrow.

I cried all morning while Mum labelled and packed Sophie's and Peter's school uniforms and books. Even Peter looked a bit glum and he *loves* boarding school (traitor!).

Peter and Sophie took me, Wes and Fez down to the dam for a picnic and yabbying. Sophie thought she looked drop-dead gorgeous in her new pink bikini until she dived into the dam and came back up with no pants and a leech stuck to her bare bum.

'Leech magnet!' yelled Fez.

'Sister of Leech Girl!' yelled Wes.

'Not my sister!' yelled Peter.

Sophie ran home crying with a piece of greaseproof paper from our sandwiches wrapped around her bum. I couldn't help feeling sorry for her. It must be hard being a fashion victim.

We caught three yabbies, twenty-seven leeches and a dead sheep. Wes and Fez put the leeches in a bowl and gave them to Miss McKenzie when she came home from school.

Peter said, 'Beware of geeks bearing gifts, Miss McKenzie.'

I think Peter might have a bit of a crush on Miss McKenzie.

Gertrude must have thought the leeches were food, because she knocked the bowl out of

Miss McKenzie's hand and gobbled them all up. Greedy pig.

I am sitting in Sophie's bed as I write this. I'm letting her braid my hair.

I will miss Peter and Sophie so much.

STINKING ROTTEN STUPID DAMNED POOEY BOARDING SCHOOL.

Tuesday, 7 February

Dad took Peter and Sophie to Bathurst this morning. I went back to bed and cried all day. In between sobs and mouthfuls of chocolate cake, I started to read *Seven Little Australians* for the two hundred and seventy-fifth time.

I tried to get Fluffles to come inside with me, but she is too busy guarding her food bowl from Gerty.

Wes and Fez spent the day in the machine shed doing something to Grandpa Weston's beaten up old Holden ute that we drive down to the bus stop.

Miss McKenzie spent the day at school.

Everyone has deserted me.

Miss McKenzie didn't get home until seven-thirty. I wonder if she and Mr Cluff are *hitting it off*, as Mum would say.

Wednesday, 8 February

We were excited about going back to school today. Actually, *I* was excited about school. Wes and Fez were excited about the new noise the old ute was making since they stuck some rubber hoses onto the end of the exhaust pipe.

I was really looking forward to seeing Mat on the bus. I had really missed her while she was at the beach. But unfortunately my best friend Mat Sweeney has turned into Matilda Jane the Mature since I saw her last. How vomitingly disappointing.

'This is our last year at Hardbake Public, Trudy! Imagine that!' she said, nudging me.

'Just one more year and we'll be off to boarding school. One — more — year … Trudy? Are you listening?'

I was still pretty upset about Peter and Sophie leaving for Bathurst yesterday, so I tried to change the subject. I don't like to think about the future, at least not when it involves boarding school. But Mat went on and on and on …

'I think it'll be great to be in Bathurst. We can get away from all these sheep and paddocks and live in a proper town with shops and cinemas and cafés … blah, blah, blah … A big school will be awesome, too ... blah, blah, blah ... heaps of girls to make friends with ... and heaps of boys!'

She giggled and nudged me again.

I can't believe it! She actually *wants* to go to boarding school!!!!

And why on earth has she started calling me Trudy? *Nobody* has called me Trudy since I grew red hair when I was eight months old!

I sat with my cheek squashed against the bus window while Mat talked on and on and on. Verbal diarrhoea I think it's called.

It was a relief when the bus pulled up outside the school and I caught sight of Miss McKenzie's curly orange hair flying around in the breeze.

I've got Mr Cluff again this year. Miss McKenzie is teaching the little kids. Let's see if she still thinks Wes and Fez are delightful when she sees them all day every day!!!

I suppose our day went pretty much like every other kid's first day back at school. Mr Cluff gave a 'Welcome back to school' speech like he does every year, telling us about his hopes for an industrious, productive, conscientious, antiseptic, superfluous, gastrointestinal year for us all, or something like that. We got new books, decorated a few title pages and wrote about what we did on the holidays. My story seemed a bit depressing, all about Dad and Peter having to shoot ninety-three starving ewes and not being able to go away at all because we'd spent all our money on water for the tank and feed for the rest of the sheep. I did end on a happier note, though, by telling the story about Miss McKenzie breaking her nose.

Home seems very lonely tonight. I am now only third to use the bath water at night — we go from oldest to youngest — and the water is so clean without Peter and Sophie ahead of me that I feel naked. I'm used to all that dirt floating around me.

Thursday, 9 February

Mat has definitely changed over the holidays. She keeps calling me Trudy even though I've told her not to, and she insists on Mr Cluff calling her Matilda Jane.

She wouldn't play soccer at lunchtime. Not even when Miss McKenzie begged her to be on her team. *Everyone* wanted to be on Miss McKenzie's team … except Mat. She just sat in the shade and smoothed her hair back behind her ears.

I feel like I have lost three people all at once — Sophie, Peter and Mat. I know Sophie and

Peter will come back at Easter, but I'm not so sure about Mat. I've read horror stories about this kind of thing. It seems that zombies have kidnapped Mat and replaced her with a lookalike called Matilda Jane the Mature. It's terrifying.

Friday, 10 February

Miss McKenzie is right at home at our school. Everybody loves her to death. She's that kind of person. She just smiles and you want to be her best friend.

I am, of course, disappointed with her nose now that the swelling has gone down, but it still has freckles like mine.

I don't remember us liking Mr Cluff so much when he first arrived. Not that we were mean or anything, although Jack Scott did bury his briefcase in the playground and Grace Simpson used to hide dominoes in his sandwiches. We just took a while to warm to him.

We all love him now, of course. He is loud and cheery, he plays soccer with us most lunch times and he never seems to get cross, not even with Wes and Fez. Mum says he must be a saint ...

Hung out with Mat at play time. She was quite chummy and I thought she might be back to normal. But when I asked her to be on my soccer team at lunch time she gave me a withering stare, sat down on the bench and started filing her nails.

WHAT HAVE YOU EVIL ZOMBIES DONE WITH MY BEST FRIEND?!?

Saturday, 11 February

Went yabbying with Wes and Fez today. We caught fifteen yabbies, twelve leeches and Sophie's pink bikini pants! I will post them to Sophie on Monday.

Wes and Fez had a leeching contest. They waded into the dam up to their waists and asked me to tell them when five minutes were up. The one with the most leeches would be the winner. Unfortunately for Wes and Fez, five minutes was just long enough for the mud to settle around their legs and they couldn't get out. They were stuck there for forty minutes until Dad came down to rescue them. By the time they got out of the dam the leeches had had a blood feast and were ENORMOUS. It was the most disgusting thing I have ever seen.

It must have been the most disgusting thing Wes and Fez have ever seen too because it really freaked them out.

Wes began to scream, 'Daddy! Daddy! Daddy! I don't wanna die!'

He was clearly hysterical, so I offered to slap him across the face, but Dad wouldn't let me.

Fez ran off home, faster than Sophie the day she lost her bikini pants, big fat leeches dangling off his legs and belly. When he got back to the house, Doris and Gertrude bailed him up and gobbled every last leech off his body.

Fez fainted!!!

Best fun I've ever had yabbying.

Sunday, 12 February

Church today. Mat and I sat up the back and giggled. The zombie lookalike must have been called back to the graveyard. Thank goodness.

Miss McKenzie joined us for Sunday lunch and has asked us to Serenity Cottage for lunch next Sunday. I hope she doesn't cook haggis!

Wrote a letter to Sophie encouraging her to run away from boarding school. Will post it with the bikini pants tomorrow.

Monday, 13 February

Mr Cluff looks like he cut his hair with a knife and fork over the weekend! Mat and I nearly died laughing in assembly. While the rest of the kids were singing 'Australia's Full of Ostriches', Mat and I were stuffing our fists in our mouths to keep ourselves from screeching hysterically.

Mat reckons Mr Cluff got caught under his lawn mower on the weekend. I reckon he's trying to impress Miss McKenzie by looking trimmed and tidy, but hasn't quite got it right yet.

Tuesday, 14 February

Miss McKenzie is going to find all the kids at school a Scottish email friend. We are all really excited. At least, I *was* excited, until Mat giggled stupidly, blushed like a tomato and said she hopes she gets a boy … a good-looking one.

I nearly chundered.

There was a really bad dust storm after lunch and we spent the rest of the day cleaning the topsoil from Mr Jackson's paddocks off our desks and books. Just as we were catching the bus home, a whole mob of sheep ran by with Mr Jackson chasing them. The wind had built the tumbleweed and dirt up against the fences like a ramp and they'd walked up out of their paddock as easy as pie, just like our sheep did.

Mum was crying when I got home. All that newspaper and foil stuffed in the cracks has stopped most of the dust getting into the house, so I don't know what her problem is.

Wednesday, 15 February

We've started planning our outdoor projects. They are the best thing about school. Every year Mr Cluff gives us a section of the schoolyard where we can do whatever we like. Well, almost. Last year Gabby Woodhouse's hairdressing salon had to close after she gave Lynette Sweeney a crew cut, and Mr Cluff didn't really like Davo Hartley and Jack Scott's snake farm idea. But most of the time we can do our own thing, as long as we stick to our own plot of land and don't waste class time.

There are always kids growing vegies and they get their plots of land side by side so the back of the schoolyard looks like a market garden. They use the recycled water from the septic system. It's meant to be totally clean, but I reckon there must still be some yuckies in it judging from the size of Sam Wotherspoon's turnips last year. He actually sent one to Guinness World Records. It cost his mum a fortune in freight and it didn't win because it had rotted by the time it arrived and looked more like something a large horse had done than a turnip.

Banjo Davies always has his Poet's Corner. He has a stack of poetry books and pencils and paper in a big old wooden chest under the schoolhouse and he sits there every lunch time, reading and writing poetry. That's why we call him Banjo. His real name's Michael.

The only time Banjo lets anyone else enter the Poet's Corner is when he holds a recital of his works — usually at Easter and in August and December. It gets pretty crowded with the whole school stuffed in under the schoolhouse, but Mr Cluff says we have to celebrate everyone's talents.

A lot of the kids are talking about getting guinea pigs, bantam hens and rabbits this year. It will be nice to be keeping something alive after seeing so many sheep die over the summer.

Not sure what I'll do. I usually grow sunflowers, but I might try something different this year.

Emailed Sophie tonight encouraging her to run away from school.

Thursday, 16 February

Harry Wilson is going to dig to China!!!!

Harry's this blocky little kid who just started kindy. He's got a crew cut — pretty much like Lynette Sweeney's hair last year — and looks as tough as nails. He's always got bruised shins and scabs on his knees.

Mr Cluff said Harry can use the recycled water from the septic system every afternoon to soak his project site. The next day the dirt will be soft and muddy and he'll be able to dig his hole. Mr Cluff is really good like that. He likes to encourage the little kids, even when their ideas are bonkers.

Wes and Fez's project is going to be a rocket launching pad! Mr Cluff said that was a great idea, but made them promise not to use real fuel. They swore they were only going to use rubber bands to catapult the rockets into the air. Mr Cluff really should know better than to believe them.

Miss McKenzie is as excited as the rest of us about the whole project thing. She spent half an hour before school digging over Tom Gillies' plot of land because she thought it would help him get started on his vegie patch. Too bad for Tom that he's trying to smooth things down to make a bowling alley!

Friday, 17 February

Lucy Ferris brought two rabbits to school today — two females, so we don't end up with a billion baby bunnies. They are living in a cardboard box until Lucy and Mr Cluff can build a proper hutch for them.

Harry Wilson is already digging to China — he's about fifty centimetres down.

Lynette Sweeney and Sarah Love were playing with the mud that Harry dug out at lunch time and got the idea of making a mud-brick house. How cool is that? I wish I'd thought of it first.

Anyway, I've decided to make a tree house. Mr Cluff gave me this perfect plot of land with a rambling old melaleuca tree in the middle of it and I'll bring in timber and nails and stuff from home. Maybe once it's built I'll start a Wes-and-Fez-Free Club! Asked Mat if she wanted to help me build it and she gave me one of her withering stares. I presume that means no. WHAT IS WRONG WITH THAT GIRL? Just when I thought she was becoming normal again.

Miss McKenzie had a big parcel delivered to her at school today. It was covered in stamps from Scotland. Wonder what it is …

Saturday, 18 February

Woken this morning by an absolutely *dreadful* noise. It started as a loud droning, picked up into an extremely loud bellow, then ended in a screech. A flock of cockatoos flew over the house squawking, and Fluffles hung off the flyscreen on my bedroom window, frozen with terror. Her eyes were as big as twenty-cent coins and her fur was puffed up all over.

Dad stomped around getting dressed. He yelled, 'If Felix Sweeney's damned bull gets caught in the barbed wire one more time I'll shoot it!'

We all followed Dad outside in our pyjamas and gumboots to investigate.

We didn't have to go far. We could just see Miss McKenzie over the top of the sheep yards, sitting in the rocking chair on her front veranda. She was wearing silky green pyjamas with a Scottish thistle pattern and she was holding a set of bagpipes! She blew into a pipe, her arm squeezed on the tartan bag and another shocking noise howled and moaned. Wes reckoned he *almost* heard a line from 'Waltzing Matilda'.

We sneaked around the sheep yards to get a closer look and saw Gertrude lying at Miss McKenzie's feet, rolling her eyes in pleasure. She

was grunting softly and wagging her tail back and forth to the screeching music.

Mum began to laugh.

Dad muttered, 'Serenity Cottage my fat ...' and went inside to make a cuppa.

Fez said he thought it sounded cool and walked over to ask Miss McKenzie for bagpipe lessons.

Mum groaned, finished Dad's sentence and followed him inside.

Sunday, 19 February

Woke again to the sound of bagpipes.

Heard Dad yell, 'If that hideous noise doesn't stop soon I'll shoot *Miss McKenzie!*'

I went outside to spy on her. I think the bagpipes sound horrible, but you have to admire someone who's brave enough to play such an instrument.

They must be so comfortable in their skin that they don't care what anyone else thinks!

Gertrude was lying at Miss McKenzie's feet again, wagging her tail and grunting softly. It was like she was singing along with the bagpipes in her own special piggy way!

Had lunch at Serenity Cottage. Miss McKenzie told Dad all about the green rolling hills back home in Scotland and how the sheep were clean and white, not brown from the dust like out here. After lunch she brought out the bagpipes, so we all decided it was time to go home. Just as we left, Gerty came running up onto the veranda to sit at Miss McKenzie's feet. That dopey pig really loves the bagpipes!

Emailed Sophie to tell her about Miss McKenzie's bagpipes and her cool silky pyjamas. Begged her to run away tomorrow. If she does she could be home by Tuesday.

Pulled three dead sheep from the dam today. Yuck!

Monday, 20 February
Bagpipes at 6 am!

Lucy Ferris's rabbits escaped from their cardboard box over the weekend, so our classroom was a sea of poo this morning. Sam Wotherspoon was so excited. He collected every last little poo ball in an ice-cream container to make compost. He has decided that this year he is going to grow the world's largest zucchini and compost is going to be the key to his success.

Spent all of recess and lunch time helping Mr Cluff and Lucy build a rabbit hutch. It's a bit wonky but the rabbits don't seem to mind. Matilda Jane, however, was not impressed at all. She doesn't even talk much any more. She just gives me one of those looks that says it all. Don't know what she's going to do with her time for the rest of the year. She can't file her fingernails every lunch time, surely? She'll end up filing her fingers down to her wrists!

Wes and Doris crashed their chariot into a barbed-wire fence this afternoon. The top of Doris's ear ripped off and was dangling from the barbed wire, until Mildred came along and ate it!!!

'Cool!' said Fez. 'Cannibal pigs!'

Tuesday, 21 February

Bagpipes at 6.05 am.

The excitement of projects has got the better of Miss McKenzie. She has taken her own plot of land in the schoolyard and declared it as the site for a mini Edinburgh Tattoo. She invited everyone to join in, and Gary Hartley and Nick Farrel volunteered straight away. They love the idea of getting a tattoo.

Harry Wilson is working like a trouper on digging to China. He's made incredible progress. He's already dug up a sheep skull, three old pennies, a chamber pot and Mr Cluff's long-lost briefcase.

Sam Wotherspoon is pestering the guts out of everyone. We'll be halfway through lunch and he's hovering around with his smelly compost bucket waiting for leftovers.

'C'mon, Blue. Don't eat all of that muffin. Save some for me compost. How 'bout you pull out the sultanas and donate 'em to a good cause.'

'Strike me lucky, Tom. Your mum doesn't give ya much tucker. How'm I ever gonna get scraps from ya if your mother doesn't feed ya properly?

Tell ya what! Gimme that fruity bar and we'll call it quits.'

'Whoa, Lucy! Lookin' a bit podgy there. Why don't ya let me look after that second sanger for ya.'

He's going to get his lights knocked out if he keeps it up!

I started building my tree house at recess today, but Wes and Fez lit a fire at lunch time and burnt all my timber and the tree!!! Now all that's left of my new project is a pile of smouldering ashes.

Wednesday, 22 February

Bagpipes at 5.59 am.

Spent the whole bus trip home from school designing tattoos with Nick and Gary. Gary made up this really awesome design for a dragon with a knife stuck in its chest which he's going to put on his shoulder. Nick just wants a love heart with 'Lynette' written in it. Miss McKenzie is so cool to let them have tattoos.

Got a letter from Sophie this afternoon. It was full of little shiny red hearts that fell into the cream on my sponge cake when I opened it. I had hoped that the letter might be postmarked somewhere between Bathurst and home, but looks like Sophie hasn't run away yet. How much encouragement does she need? Maybe if I hadn't posted her bikini pants she would have come home to get them.

Thursday, 23 February

Bagpipes at 6.03 am.

It turns out that this Edinburgh Tattoo doesn't have anything at all to do with tattoos! It's a big parade in Scotland with singing and dancing and BAGPIPES.

Gary and Nick are so disappointed, but they're too much in love with Miss McKenzie to let her down. They spent all of lunch time marching, dancing and singing 'My Bonnie Lies Over the Ocean'. It sounded horrible.

Mr Cluff did one of his Big Wide World lessons today. He sounded just like Mum. He said he wants to teach us that Hardbake Plains is *not* the centre of the universe and that there are millions of opportunities out there for us. I actually believe that Hardbake Plains *is* the centre of the universe. Maybe not for the president of Russia, the minke whale or Madonna, but it is for me. Nevertheless, I pretended that the Bake was *not* the centre of my whole life — past, present and future — until Mr Cluff's lesson ended.

Our big thing for this term is ferreting through newspapers. Today we read articles on global warming, ethnic wars, bird flu, famine and the stock market. Mr Cluff was very careful to explain that the stock market was *not* a place where you sold your fat lambs and heifers.

By three o'clock our notice board was covered in headlines:

'ENOUGH IS ENOUGH!' SHOUTS PM

EGGS CAUSE CANCER

Middle East peace talks grind to a halt

Girl power surges

INDUSTRIAL STRIFE BRINGS MELBOURNE TO ITS KNEES

Who cares? What about:

DROUGHT DRIVES TOUGH MOTHER TO TEARS

or

Farmer shoots eighteen starving sheep

or

Twin boys disappear mysteriously from farm — Police suspect fed-up sister of foul play.

Dad *did* have to shoot eighteen sheep today.

Friday, 24 February

Bagpipes at 6.10 am.

We now have four guinea pigs, two rabbits and seven bantam hens at school. Sam is ecstatic about all the poo. He has planted six zucchinis and is smothering them in compost.

Wes and Fez launched their first rocket today. Well, the rocket itself stayed firmly on the ground, but the base flew at least twenty metres into the air. Quite impressive considering they only used rubber bands.

This Edinburgh Tattoo thing is going to be torture. Miss McKenzie let Gary play her bagpipes today and Lucy's rabbits went crazy. They ran around and around in circles making a weird screaming noise. It was quite disturbing.

Saturday, 25 February

Mrs Whittington has returned!

The Country Women's Association put on a big afternoon tea today to welcome her home.

Mrs Whittington has been secretary of the CWA since dinosaurs became extinct. She lives next to the pub, but she's spent the last six months in a nursing home in Dubbo because she has Alzheimer's Disease. Her son Bob reckons she's a danger to herself and others living all alone, but she isn't. She can look after herself, her house and chooks and she's happy. Anyway, people in the Bake look out for her. She just forgets to do things from time to time, like getting dressed before she goes to the shop, or taking her shoes off before she puts her gumboots on — nothing that anyone around here cares about.

Mrs Whittington hated living in the nursing home. She said they fed her and dressed her and talked to her as if she was a baby, and she missed her chooks and all her friends in Hardbake Plains. So last Tuesday night, when the nurses thought she was sleeping, she got dressed (*three* times, but that doesn't matter) and ran away. She hitchhiked all the way back home.

Everyone was so glad to see her again. You know how your bed just doesn't seem right without your old, floppy pillow, or a cup of tea just doesn't seem right without that third teaspoon full of sugar? Well, Hardbake Plains just didn't seem right without Mrs Whittington.

Sunday, 26 February

Stinking hot today so Wes, Fez and I went swimming in the pathetic puddle of water that's left in the dam. We got twenty-one leeches. Wes insisted on keeping them stuck to us until we got home where he plucked them free and put them in a jar for Show and Tell.

Fez must still be a little bit traumatised by the last leech episode. He cried all the way home and vomited when Wes pulled a big orange-and-black striped leech off his arm!

Miss McKenzie has been in Dubbo all weekend. Gertrude went crazy when she got home. She chased after her like a frisky puppy — a very large, blubbery puppy — and wouldn't settle until Miss McKenzie played the bagpipes.

I wonder if other peoples' lives are as whacko as ours ...

Monday, 27 February

Bagpipes at 6.02 am.

Wes took his leeches into school for Show and Tell. Unfortunately he SHOWED before he TELLED and Ben Simpson shoved one in his mouth before Wes explained that they were leeches, not liquorice.

Having Mrs Whittington back in town is going to be better than I thought! About a year ago, the CWA held an essay competition on the subject of country life. I wrote a very passionate essay on the importance of bush schools and how evil boarding school is because it takes children away from their birthplace, separates families and steals future farmers from the land. It really was quite brilliant for a ten-year-old. I won first prize, a leather-bound copy of *Seven Little Australians*. Very appropriate!

Mrs Whittington loved my essay and said she'd bake me my favourite cake as a reward. I asked her for steamed golden syrup pudding — not technically a cake, but well worth sinking your teeth into. She brought the pudding to school the very next day, and continued to bring one every two or three weeks after that because she kept forgetting that she'd already made one for me. Each time she'd smile and say, 'I've finally made that pudding that I promised you, Blue. Lovely essay, darling. The bush is the heart of our beautiful country. Well done. Well done. Enjoy the pudding.'

And we did — every single time!!!

I felt a bit guilty at first and was going to remind her that she'd already made me a pudding, but Mr Cluff said not to. He said it made Mrs Whittington happy … and it sure made *us* happy, so why mess with something good?

Anyway, Mrs Whittington turned up at school today during music with Miss McKenzie. She was wearing her sheepskin slippers and woolly socks — even though it was thirty-nine degrees outside — and had a freshly steamed GOLDEN SYRUP PUDDING with her. She'd even made a bowl of custard.

'Sorry I've taken so long to make it for you, Blue,' she said. 'Lovely essay, darling. The bush is the heart of our beautiful country. Well done. Well done. Enjoy the pudding.'

Miss McKenzie is lovely. She didn't seem to think there was anything weird about an old lady turning up at school with sheepskin slippers and a pudding. She just asked Mrs Whittington to join our lesson and was really excited when she found out that Mrs W used to play the piano for dances at the town hall. Miss McKenzie pulled out her bagpipes (she never seems to notice that we groan when she starts to play) and we sang everything from 'The Wild Colonial Boy' to 'Get the Party Started', accompanied by the piano and the bagpipes. It was the first time the bagpipes sounded okay —

probably because the piano and all us kids drowned them out a bit.

Miss McKenzie and Mrs Whittington played songs right through our lunch break. They really hit it off together and kept getting noisier and sillier.

Miss McKenzie's amazing. She can play the bagpipes and laugh at the same time. And she still looks lovely.

Mrs Whittington finally had to go home because her feet were getting too hot.

Tuesday, 28 February

Bagpipes at 6.00 am on the dot.

Mr Cluff is really getting into this Big Wide World thing. We're reading newspapers every day and cutting out headlines like our lives depended on it. Our notice board is getting a bit crowded and some of the headlines are starting to overlap. The oddest things are beginning to happen in the world:

Terrorist threat to THE GREAT AUSSIE MEAT PIE

ENDANGERED WHALES take to the streets in protest

NUCLEAR TESTING in childcare centres

Zoo's new baby gorilla **EMITS POISONOUS GASES**

71

Talking about poisonous gases, Sam's compost pile is *enormous*. He's been bringing in bags of sheep droppings from his farm and just about steals the poo from the guinea pigs and the rabbits before it hits the ground. His zucchinis are surrounded by such a massive mountain of compost that you can barely see them.

Wes and Fez have been suspiciously quiet on the rocket front. I've read about the natural phenomenon of the calm before the storm. Makes me nervous …

March

Wednesday, 1 March

Barely noticed the bagpipes at 6.05 am. They are becoming part of the morning sounds around here, together with the cockatoos squawking and the rooster crowing.

They are also becoming a part of Gertrude's routine. Gerty lies on the veranda of Serenity Cottage every morning, waiting for Miss McKenzie. Miss McKenzie comes out in her pyjamas, plays a bagpipe tune or two (or three if we're really unlucky!), gives a piece of shortbread or a chocolate bickie to Gertrude, and has a cup of tea herself. Weird as!

I was flicking through the newspapers during our Big Wide World lesson today when I found an article about the Sultan of Brughistan. He's one of the richest men in the world and he owns hundreds of oil wells. Out here we'd rather have *water* in our wells, but this Sultan bloke seems to be doing okay. He owns three marble palaces, eight yachts, a stretch limousine with a spa in the back (!!!!!), enough famous artworks to fill a gallery and fifty racehorses.

It was the bit about the horses that interested me the most. This article said that the Sultan of Brughistan buys the best hay in the whole wide world for his horses and he has heaps and heaps and heaps of it. I reckon he probably has enough hay to carry every farmer in the state through the drought.

Hmmmmm … maybe I'll write to him …

After all, Mr Cluff is always telling us to expand our horizons …

Thursday, 2 March

Matilda Jane the Mature strikes again.

Mat gave her guinea pig to Lucy Ferris at recess today and when Lucy asked her its name, Mat said she hadn't got around to naming it. Who has a guinea pig for three weeks and doesn't even name it??? Matilda Jane the Mature, that's who!

Then at lunch time, Sam asked Mat for her banana skin and she told him he was childish.

Davo Hartley said, 'Well, duh. That would be because he *is* a child.'

Didn't *that* make Mat livid? She threw her banana skin at Davo and screamed that it was time we all grew up. Lynette was so upset she wet her pants. Harry Wilson said he'd think about growing up when he turned six, but right now he was too busy digging to China. Banjo Davies rubbed his chin thoughtfully and then disappeared under the schoolhouse to write a poem about schoolyard conflict.

Tonight I told Mum about Mat and how weird she was getting and how I thought that maybe she doesn't like me any more. It's not much fun feeling like you're losing your best friend. Mum said I should invite Mat to come and play for the weekend, but I'm not so sure. I'll think about it.

Read through the newspaper article about the Sultan of Brughistan again. Think I'll dream of mountains of golden hay tonight. Imagine being so lucky!

Friday, 3 March

When we got to school this morning there was a poem stuck up on the gate:

Matilda got so angry
She threw a banana skin.
It flew through the sky
And hit Davo on the chin.
Matilda screamed at everyone.
Lynette cried and peed.
Stop playground violence!
Peace is what we need.

It was signed, 'Local Poet for Peace'.

Banjo must have been very moved by Mat's performance yesterday. He doesn't usually share any of his poems before an official recital.

Lynette was very excited about being in a real poem. Matilda the Mature ripped the poem down and stomped it into Sam's compost pile. Unfortunately for Mat, the compost had started to break down, so her leg sank deep down into greeny-brown putrid sludge.

Banjo nodded wisely and said, 'Poetic justice.'

Saturday, 4 March

Watched a show about stunt motorcyclists on TV this afternoon. Mum freaked when she realised that Wes and Fez had watched a whole hour of people riding motorbikes through hoops of fire and over buses. Dad said it was better than them watching the special on the ABC about the damned drought.

Mum looked really old and sad tonight at dinner. Wes and Fez must have noticed, because they made her tea and toast for supper and called her Mummy Darling Heart and promised never to be naughty ever again. We all know they can't keep that promise, but it cheered Mum up anyway.

Sunday, 5 March

Fez broke his collarbone again this afternoon. Wes got concussion.

Fez came running into the house wearing Sophie's old pink tutu, his left arm dangling oddly by his side, screaming and crying, 'Wes is dead! Wes is dead! Mummy! Mummy! Wes is dead as a doornail!'

We ran outside and found Wes, totally unconscious, wedged between a dead sheep and a forty-four gallon drum. He was wearing a stack hat and his green Incredible Hulk undies over his shorts. Doris was lying on the ground beside him with the chariot on top of her. She could've stood up and walked

away but she's too lazy. She never wants to go anywhere unless there's food waiting for her.

Wes and Fez had been trying to break the Guinness World Record for the largest number of wheelbarrows, forty-four gallon drums and dead sheep to be jumped by a pig and chariot. Fez, a.k.a. Pinky Pus Buster, had gone first, but Mildred had chickened out and stopped suddenly at the top of the ramp. Pinky had been thrown out of the chariot and onto the edge of a wheelbarrow — broken collarbone. Wes, a.k.a. the Green Daredevil, didn't notice (or chose not to notice) Pinky Pus Buster's screams of agony and let rip with Doris. Doris, it seems, was braver (or dumber) than Mildred and took the jump — severe concussion for the Green Daredevil.

Mum didn't even bother to call Mr Sweeney. She said she's dealt with enough broken bones and concussions to start a specialist practice.

Wes and Fez are stoked because they can't go to school tomorrow.

Monday, 6 March

Wrote my letter to the Sultan of Brughistan today. Here it is:

Dear Mr Sultan of Brughistan,

How are you? I am very well, although I have a cold sore on my lip at the moment. At least it takes people's attention away from my wide nose and big feet for a while.

It must be lovely being so rich. I suppose you go to the movies quite a bit and don't even have to worry about patching your jeans when the knees get holes. You are very lucky.

You are especially lucky to have enough hay to feed your horses for the next 500 years.

Here at Hardbake Plains we are not so fortunate. We have had a terribly bad drought for over three years and there's not a blade of grass in the paddocks. There's not even much dirt in the paddocks any more. Most of it has blown away! All of the farmers are very poor. They haven't had a wheat crop for years and they've spent every last cent on food for their sheep, water for their tanks and dams, and bullets for their guns. The bullets are to put the starving sheep out of their misery. My dad has shot 270 sheep so far and will probably have to kill a lot more before this damned drought is over (pardon my French!). He has to dig huge holes to bury them all.

Which brings me to my question. I was wondering if you could spare any of that hay? It doesn't even have to be the good stuff. Any old hay will do. I know it's for your horses but the sheep around here aren't too fussy at the moment. Neither are the farmers.

I hope you don't think it's rude of me to ask and please don't tell my mum. She often says my manners are despicable.

If you do send some hay, I will send you my mum's recipe for steamed golden syrup pudding. You really haven't lived until you've tasted it. But you have to eat it with cream and custard made with very fresh eggs. I'm sure your wife will be able to make it for you — Mum says it's a foolproof recipe.

Yours sincerely,

Trudy Alice Weston
(But you can call me Blue if you send the hay)

I posted it and gave Mr Cluff a copy as part of my Big Wide World project for the term. I know it won't come to anything, but it felt good writing it. It's fun to imagine all the farmers getting a big break and it can't do any harm, can it?

Tuesday, 7 March

Mrs Whittington brought me another golden syrup pudding today. Mat and I sat on the steps eating it straight from the bowl while we watched Harry Wilson digging to China.

Harry's digging at an amazing rate. You can only see from his shoulders up when he's in the hole, and he's digging up so much dirt now that Lynette and Sarah can't even use it all for their mud-brick house. He's been piling it up on Davo Hartley and Jack Scott's plot and I think they're going to build a BMX track.

Wes and Fez spent all day in bed making rockets. They have a plastic crate full of fan belts (nicked from Dad's workshop), rubber bands, old jock elastic, stockings and hair elastics. By the time I got home, they had two rockets stuck in the mud walls of their bedroom and Fez had a black eye.

Wednesday, 8 March

It would seem that Matilda Jane the Mature has gone on holidays and left my good old friend Mat behind.

HALLELUJAH!

Mat and I helped Lynette and Sarah make mud bricks at recess, and Mat even played soccer with us at lunch time. If Mat the Normal is still alive and well tomorrow, I'll ask her to stay at Hillrose Poo this weekend.

Mrs Whittington has started visiting the school in between puddings, just to spend time with Miss McKenzie. They sit on the veranda at lunch time and gossip and giggle. Miss McKenzie loves to hear about Hardbake Plains in the olden days when Mrs Whittington was Miss Wool and Wheat at the Harvest Festival five years in a row. Mrs Whittington loves to hear all about Scotland, where the grass is green and the sheep are white.

Thursday, 9 March
Another day, another dust storm.

Mum was crying again when I got home. The house didn't seem too dusty. I suppose she's just fed up.

I hate it when Mum cries. Mums and dads aren't meant to cry, but I reckon quite a few around here have had a quiet sniffle or two lately.

Friday, 10 March
Sam Wotherspoon's zucchini plants are dead. I think they suffocated in sheep poo. Sam does,

however, have enough compost to fill an Olympic size swimming pool and he is very proud of this.

Davo and Jack are making the coolest BMX track. All the kids are talking about bringing their bikes to school on the bus next week. I just hope Wes and Fez don't try to bring Mildred and Doris along to do their stunts!

Mat agreed to come over for the weekend. I'm really excited. Mat and I always have a great time when she comes to Hillrose Park. We build cubbies in the peppercorn trees, chase sheep, watch cartoons and sneak around the kitchen in the middle of the night making pikelets and chocolate crackles and all sorts of yummy midnight feasts. Sometimes we write plays and perform them for Mum and Dad. I suppose I'll have to do the make-up and hairdressing thing as well, but that's okay. I can do that for a good friend.

Mrs Sweeney is dropping Mat over in the morning.

Sunday, 12 March

Oh brother! What a weekend! We've just dropped Mat home, or was it Matilda Jane the Mature? I'm really not sure!

When Mat arrived yesterday, she didn't want to do the usual stuff. Every time I suggested something fun, like a drive around the dams to check on the sheep, or a picnic on the garage roof, she just stared at me with her chest sticking out (which I'm sure, by the way, she'd padded up with tissues) or rolled her eyes. She was completely unimpressed with the chariot Wes and Fez are making for Miss McKenzie (and it really *is* impressive — they've even carved a pattern of Scottish thistles into the timber). She wouldn't make slingshots to shoot the rats in the hayshed and she nearly fainted at the mention of a midnight feast.

'Don't you care about your figure?' she asked. 'I'd just *die* if I got another pimple!'

She just wanted to look at Sophie's fashion magazines and try on clothes. So that's what we did … ALL DAY LONG!!! She talked about boys ALL THE TIME, and not even the boys at our school! She spent hours and hours talking about GAVIN O'DONNELL, who's in Peter's year at boarding school. I mean, really! HE'S OLD ENOUGH TO BE HER BROTHER!!!!! But Mat just wouldn't shut up about him …

'Gavin has beautiful brown eyes.'

'Gavin is going to be a lawyer. He'll make *such* a good lawyer.'

'Gavin will soon be home for Easter holidays.'

'I wonder whether Gavin likes girls to have short hair or long hair?'

I told Mat that we used to have a goat called Gavin who could fart so loudly he'd wake  us all up in the middle of the night from three paddocks away. Matilda Jane gave me one of her withering stares and told me I was childish. She said that I needed to grow up because at boarding school next year people would be doing far more mature things with their time than talking about farting goats.

I said that I certainly hoped *not*, and that painting your fingernails purple, piercing your ears with safety pins and fainting over Gavin O'Donnell's new hairdo was hardly mature. Mat walked off in a huff and I couldn't find her for ages.

I went over to Serenity Cottage to see if Miss McKenzie knew where Mat was. Miss McKenzie looked so lovely and friendly with her freckly nose and wrinkly, smiley face that I burst into tears. I told her all about the fight we'd had. She started to play a tune on her bagpipes to cheer me up, so I left to look for Mat.

I finally found her in the peppercorn tree, eating scones with jam and cream. Doris, Mildred and Gerty were standing below her, drooling and snorting greedily.

I told her she'd get pimples.

She offered me one and said we'd get pimples together and I knew that she meant sorry … for now at least.

I spent the rest of the weekend designing wedding dresses (?!?) and changing hairdos until Mat went home. I even wore a mini skirt and three bracelets to church this morning, which meant that I couldn't play cricket with the other kids while the mums and dads had a cuppa.

Now I'm going out into the shed with Wes and Fez to make cubbies in the hay bales and do some rat spotlighting and JUST BE NORMAL.

Monday, 13 March

Miss McKenzie has really upped the Edinburgh Tattoo rehearsals. She's planning a performance for the whole school on the last day of term. She and Nick and Gary played the bagpipes all lunch time and I still have a splitting headache.

Wes and Fez are going berserk making rockets. They launched one at school today. It hit Lynette Sweeney in the face and gave her a bleeding nose, so Nick Farrel hit Wes in the face and gave *him* a bleeding nose!

Mat sighed and said, 'How romantic.'

Tuesday, 14 March

Got our first emails from our Scottish email friends today. Mr Cluff is more excited than any of us. He says it is yet another way to broaden our horizons.

Mat obviously doesn't want to broaden her horizons. She was really peeved because she was dead set on getting a good-looking boy who would propose to her and carry her off to his castle in Scotland on a white stallion but instead she got a buck-toothed girl whose hobbies are stamp collecting and trout fishing. Mat deleted her email and spent the afternoon looking at some lame website about supermodels!

My email friend is called Katrina Douglass and she looks really nice. She lives on a farm where they have these really hairy cows called Scottish longhorns and she has four-year-old triplet brothers. Wes and Fez are bad enough. Imagine if there was a third one!!!

Wednesday, 15 March

Miss McKenzie's Belch Bag Band had another rehearsal today. Things are sounding really bad. I noticed that Mr Cluff has started bringing earplugs to school in his lunchbox. But, as Mrs Whittington would say, every cloud has a silver lining. Miss McKenzie has started teaching Nick and Gary the Highland fling, and it is funnier than watching the clowns at the circus. Nick dances at a forty-five degree angle, so he always looks like he's about to fall over, but amazingly he never does. Gary falls over all the time.

Banjo watched for a while then crawled off under the schoolhouse mumbling, 'The Highland fling, the Highland fling. What a truly wondrous thing.'

Thursday, 16 March

Bob Whittington turned up this morning with two nurses to take Mrs Whittington back to the nursing home. Luckily Miss McKenzie saw him out the window of her classroom and rang Mrs Murphy, the president of the CWA. Before too long six CWA women, Mr Murphy and four men from the Bush Fire Brigade had arrived and chased Bob and the nurses away. Bob tried to get back in the house to see Mrs Whittington but Mr Murphy stood in the doorway and stared him down.

The Bake's like that. People stick together through thick and thin.

Friday, 17 March

Got an email from Katrina Douglass today. It is snowing on her farm at the moment! It's hard to imagine when it's thirty-six degrees and blazing sunshine over here.

I emailed her a few photos of our dusty farm and filthy, starving sheep.

Saturday, 18 March

Dad shot four more sheep today and I found one dead in the dam.

Mum sat on the veranda all afternoon staring at the bill for Sophie and Peter's school fees. Fluffles jumped up on Mum's lap and coughed a huge, slimy furball up on the bill, but Mum didn't even crack a smile.

I'm starting to freak out.

Sunday, 19 March

Mum, Miss McKenzie and I went over to the Sweeneys' to play tennis this afternoon. Mat and Miss McKenzie beat me and Mum six–love. Mum and I usually make a good team, but Mum didn't seem very focused today.

Mat and I had a really good talk in her bedroom before I went home. I told Mat about Mum and all the crying. Mat said her dad went over to the Hartleys' farm the other day to help Davo and Gary's dad put a whole heap of starving sheep out of their misery and when he came home he shut himself in the bathroom for three hours. He didn't talk to any of them until the next morning and then he drank a glass of whisky with his breakfast before he went out to help the Gillies with some sheep.

I'm really starting to freak out now. I wish Sophie and Peter were home.

Monday, 20 March

Grace Simpson jumped down into Harry's hole at recess. Harry turned on the septic pump and flooded Grace out with recycled water. Harry doesn't like anyone interfering with his dig to China. He's so serious about it all. Grace's feet smelled really bad for the rest of the day.

Got an email from Katrina. She thanked me for the photos and said she really admired my good English and computer skills because I must have had a lot of obstacles to overcome growing up in a Third World country.

Third World country?!?!?

I deleted the email and Miss Highland Katrina with her green meadows and clean, hairy cows and stormed off to find Mat.

We both had a good laugh over the buck-toothed, trout-fishing stamp collector and the hairy-cowed ignoramus. Maybe I've been too

tough on Mat lately. After all, she *was* right about the Scottish twits.

Tuesday, 21 March

Had the day off school today. Mum and Dad had to see the bank manager in Dubbo — and I don't think it was a joyous occasion. Late last night I overheard Dad muttering something about mortgages and going bankrupt, and Mum sniffling about decent clothes for me, Wes and Fez. I don't know why she'd be worried about that! All I need is a sturdy pair of gumboots for working around the farm, and Wes and Fez would just ruin any new clothes by tearing them on barbed wire, trees and pigs' teeth.

After two hours at the bank we called in on Mr Ashmore at the hardware store where he works now. He didn't really look like he belonged. He's the sort of bloke who looks naked without his work boots and hat and a bit of dry grass hanging out the side of his mouth.

We told him all about renaming Bacon, Sausage and Salami and the pig racing and stunt action. He laughed so much when I told him about Gertrude and the bagpipes, I thought he was going to have a heart attack. Afterwards he looked as though he was going to cry. Mum gave him a big hug.

Dad slapped him on the back and said the drought had to end soon. It always rains after a drought. But Mr Ashmore said it hadn't ended soon enough for his family.

Just as we were leaving, Mr Ashmore handed Wes and Fez a big bag of pipes, rubber tubing and hoses. He winked and said that they were offcuts he'd been saving. He thought Wes and Fez might find something fun to do with them.

Good grief!

Wednesday, 22 March

Wes and Fez are working overtime making rockets out of all that stuff Mr Ashmore gave them. They've got a whole shoebox full of heavy-duty elastic bands to catapult the rockets into the air. At the end of lunch they put on a rocket-launching display for the whole school. All five rockets stayed firmly on the ground while their launching pads flew into the air. Unfortunately the fifth launching pad flew quite a distance and hit Mat in the side of the head, breaking her new hair clip. She sure was cross!

I tried to get her to see the funny side of things but she let rip and called me the most immature teenager ever to have walked the earth. I pointed out that I was only eleven and therefore not *technically* a teenager. She gave me one of her withering stares and stormed off.

Poor Banjo was frantically recording the whole argument, thinking it might be good poetry material, when Mat stormed past and whacked his notepad out of his hand and into Sam's compost heap. Banjo walked off to his poetry corner muttering, 'Matilda … killed her … Mat … splat …' Obviously, he deals with his emotions through his poetry. He didn't come out until school was over and the bus arrived.

Thursday, 23 March

Mr Jackson's back paddock ended up smeared all over our desks and books again today. His sheep escaped onto the racetrack behind the school, so Mr Cluff sent Tom, Jack and Davo over to help round them up.

Got an email from Sophie saying that because

she'd be home for Easter in two weeks' time, there was no point in running away now.

I beg to differ!

Spent four hours emailing a whole chapter of *Seven Little Australians* to her.

Friday, 24 March

Banjo invited me into his poet's corner at lunch time!!! No-one ever gets to visit his writing spot, except for the three recitals each year. He was having trouble with some rhyming and asked me in to help because I'm the best at English in the school.

He was still mad at Mat for flinging his notepad into Sam's compost and was trying to find a word that rhymed with Matilda that meant craziest lunatic girl in the universe. Not an easy thing to do, although I did point out that 'Mat' rhymed with 'fat' and 'brat' and 'Sweeney' rhymed with 'meany'.

It was quite cosy under the schoolhouse and it was fun to be working with a fellow writer. I told Banjo about my diary and how I wrote in it every day, hoping that one day it would be famous like William Wills' diary.

Banjo pointed out that Wills' diary was famous because he was a great explorer, who endured incredibly harsh conditions and soldiered on even when there was little hope of survival. I pointed out that with Wes and Fez as brothers, *I* was constantly enduring harsh conditions and had little hope of survival, so my chances of fame and glory were looking promising.

Saturday, 25 March

Dad came in tonight after shooting eleven sheep and stomped around the house, shouting and banging doors and yelling at Wes and Fez and me. Mum made him a cup of tea, as though that would solve all his problems, and it did seem to calm him down a bit.

When he'd finished his cuppa he said we needed to do something fun, so we're going to celebrate Easter with a bang this year, by letting our hair down and kicking our heels up. Mum wondered if our heels would get tangled in our hair and trip us up if we did both at once but Dad said that would just add to the fun.

So we're going to have a big bonfire and invite the Simpsons, the Sweeneys, the O'Donnells, the Hartleys, Mr Cluff and Miss McKenzie. Mum is going to cook up a storm and Dad is going to dust off his old violin and ask Mr Sweeney and

Mrs Hartley to bring their guitars. I noticed that no-one mentioned Miss McKenzie bringing her bagpipes. Wes and Fez said they'd make a fantastic rocket display. At least if Mr Sweeney is there he can stitch up any casualties straight away!

It's the most excited I've seen Mum and Dad about anything for months. Dad was actually singing in the bath tonight. It sounded really bad. Gertrude lay at the back door wagging her tail and grunting happily, just like she does when Miss McKenzie plays the bagpipes.

Sunday, 26 March

Miss McKenzie called over this afternoon to borrow a cup of sugar for some biscuits she was baking FOR GERTRUDE!!!!! Each morning, before breakfast, Miss McKenzie continues to bring her bagpipes out onto the veranda of Serenity Cottage and shatter our peace and quiet with a tune. On a *good* day it sounds like cats being strangled while an angle grinder cuts through heavy steel. Gertrude lies at Miss McKenzie's feet and grunts happily. She stares up at her, eyelashes fluttering, and snuffles softly to the music. Miss McKenzie feeds her a biscuit then disappears inside for breakfast. Gerty stays on the veranda for a while, humming the tune over and over again in her thick, porky head.

Every evening, as the sun sets, Gertrude shuffles up to the veranda once more and waits for Miss McKenzie to bring the bagpipes outside for a bedtime song. If Miss McKenzie is late, Gerty gets agitated. She paces back and forth along the veranda, snorting and squealing in that horrible way that only pigs and bagpipes can manage. She's an addict for sure. The bagpipes are to Gerty what air is to the rest of us.

Poor pig.

Miss McKenzie stopped for a while this afternoon and helped me and Mum decorate the invitations to our Easter party. Unfortunately she's going to Sydney for the school break and won't be able to come to the bonfire. Why would she want to go to Sydney when she could spend Easter at the farm? Miss McKenzie is lovely, but sometimes she's a bit odd.

Monday, 27 March

I'm writing this in Banjo's poet's corner. It's a bit dark for writing, but at least it's quiet away from the playground. Half the kids have brought their bikes to school on the bus so they can use Davo and Jack's BMX track. They've made some huge stunt jumps from all the mud Harry Wilson has dug up.

I'm really starting to believe Harry might actually make it to China at the rate he's going. He conned his mum into buying him a miner's helmet with a headlamp. Now he walks into school at the start of the day looking like he's clocking on to work the coalmines.

Banjo is putting the finishing touches to his poems for his Easter recital on the last day of term.

Tuesday, 28 March

Lucy's rabbits had eight babies over night. Guess they weren't two females after all.

Sam is beside himself. More rabbits means more poo and now he's working towards getting the Guinness World Record for the biggest pile of compost. Is there actually a Guinness World Record for the biggest pile of compost? If there was a record for the biggest lunatic, Sam might be in with a chance ... although he'd have to fight Matilda Jane the Mature for the title.

Wednesday, 29 March

Wes and Fez were watching the synchronised swimming on TV when I came into the lounge room after dinner tonight. Weird ... They're into violent stuff like stunt driving, American football, ice hockey, wrestling and boxing. What has synchronised swimming got to do with anything???

Thursday, 30 March

Thought Mat was being all normal today when she told me how much she was looking forward to our Easter party. I was planning our strategy for hide-and-seek in the dark so we could beat the boys for once, when Mat rudely interrupted with something about manicures and whether Gavin O'Donnell was likely to prefer red or purple nail polish on his women.

Women??? WOMEN!!!!!!!

Ground control to Mat ...

Blurghhh ... (That was me vomiting.)

Friday, 31 March

Only six days until Sophie and Peter return to the fold. Only six days until they are restored to their rightful place at Hillrose Poo. Six days and our family will be perfect again.

Well, we can never really be perfect with Wes and Fez here, but if they get swept away in a violent dust storm before next Thursday, my life will be perfect.

Peter is bringing his best friend, Xiu, home for Easter. Xiu's Chinese and his mother and father live in Malaysia. They send him to boarding school in Bathurst so he'll learn good English. It's too expensive for him to fly home every holiday, so he often comes to Hillrose Park with Peter.

Xiu's really cool. He loves coming to the farm and he fits in like one of the family. Mum tries to cook Malaysian food while he's here, but really he prefers lamb chops and lamingtons.

Dad likes Xiu because he's strong and will work like a trouper all day long with him and Peter.

Wes and Fez love Xiu because his parents own a pyrotechnics company in Kuala Lumpur. Xiu always comes loaded with firecrackers.

April

Saturday, 1 April

SYNCHRONISED ROCKET LAUNCHING!!!

I knew there was something fishy going on.

Wes and Fez have seventeen rockets in the shearing shed, all ready for their end-of-term synchronised rocket launch at school. I was going to tell Mum but she seems so happy at the moment, preparing for the Easter party and Sophie and Peter coming home, I didn't want to bother her.

Five days until Sophie and Peter return.

Sunday, 2 April

Wes and Fez used four of their rockets to do a practice synchronised rocket launch. It worked beautifully. All four rockets flew through the air in perfect synch, so when they smashed through the windscreen on the old Holden ute it was impossible to tell which rocket had shattered the glass first. Very impressive.

We haven't told Dad yet. Don't think he'll see the funny side of having to pay for more repairs. Wes and Fez have used two rolls of cling wrap to make a new windscreen. It actually feels pretty tough, but you can't *see* through it. Should make driving to the bus stop tomorrow interesting.

Four days until Sophie and Peter come home!!!!

Monday, 3 April

I'm lucky to be alive! Wes drove the old ute down to the bus stop without being able to see a thing. If you had to supply a whole army with packed sandwiches the windscreen would come in very handy, but if you need to see the road for driving it is totally useless! Fez stuck his head out the window and directed Wes with his steering — 'A little bit to the left … no … turn a bit to the right …' I was just about to point out that neither of them knows their left from their right, when Wes drove so close to the old tractor wreck that the driver's side door handle was torn completely off. I got out and walked the rest of the way.

When we got to school Mr Cluff was trying for the Hardbake Plains Public School record for the fastest circuit of Jack and Davo's BMX stunt track. He went so fast that he became airborne over quite a few of the jumps. Miss McKenzie clocked him at thirty-five seconds, the new official record!

Mr Cluff staggered off to class looking as though he'd just ridden from Broome to Bathurst on horseback.

Davo nodded wisely to Jack and said, 'Bike bum.'

Mr Cluff sat on a cushion for the rest of the day.

Three days until Sophie and Peter come home. I am busting!

Tuesday, 4 April

I feel sick.

No, I feel worse than sick.

I feel like someone has taken a wheelbarrow load of cement and poured it into my stomach and now it is sitting there like a heavy block that is weighing me down.

When we got home from school today there were two things lying on the dining table. One was a letter from the bank filled with words like, 'We regret to inform you,' and, 'debt,' and, 'long overdue,' and stating an unbelievably enormous amount of money. The other was a newspaper, which was open to the employment section and had three different job ads circled in red pen. One was for a builder's labourer and two were for factory workers. None of them was anywhere near Hardbake Plains.

Mum came in while I was gawking at the papers. She sighed and tried to put her arm around me, but I ran out and hid in the machine shed. I sat there and cried until it was dark.

Wednesday, 5 April

Mum and Dad came into my bedroom late last night and we had a long talk. Dad said he's looking for a job away from home, just to get enough money to keep things together until the drought is over. If the job is close enough to Hillrose Park, he'll still be home most weekends.

I tried to tell them that the farm needed Dad all the time, but Mum said that she'll look after things and Mr Sweeney will come over to help with the big jobs. Wes, Fez and I can help a lot too. What she doesn't seem to get is that *we* need Dad here all the time. It's bad enough that Sophie and Peter have gone away without us losing Dad too.

I tried to remind them how sad and lost Mr Ashmore looks now that he's away from his farm, but Dad said this is different. He isn't leaving for good, just for a short while until things get back to normal on the farm.

I cried so hard and for so long that I didn't get to sleep until sunrise. When I woke up, the bus had gone and Mum said I should have the day at home with her. Dad had already left to go job hunting and wouldn't be back until tomorrow, after he picked Sophie, Peter and Xiu up from Bathurst.

Now it's just Mum, Wes, Fez and me. Thank goodness Miss McKenzie is at Serenity Cottage. Shame about the bagpipes.

Thursday, 6 April

We sure ended the term with a bang today.

Or should I say with a smash?

Wes and Fez lined ten rockets up side by side for a synchronised rocket launch and let 'em rip. Seven of the rockets stayed firmly on the ground, while their launching pads flew into the air — sending everyone running for cover. One rocket flew into Sam's compost heap and disappeared. Another rocket looped backwards and hit Wes in the face. The tenth rocket travelled at least sixty metres, because that's how far it is from our project area to the classroom, where it smashed through the window.

We were all really impressed. Wes and Fez were disappointed though. They wanted the rockets to fly gracefully, accurately, side by side, and if they couldn't do that, they at least wanted sparks and flames and whooshing noises, and you can't get any of those with just rubber bands for launching power. Those boys are never satisfied.

Banjo crammed us all into the space under the schoolhouse for his latest poetry recital. Some of his poems were pretty good, but he won't let me write them into my diary because he wants to publish them on his own one day.

'How would Banjo Paterson have liked it if the world had first read his poems in Wills' diary?' he asked me. He's got a point there, although it would have been an *amazing* achievement seeing as Banjo Paterson wasn't born until three years after Wills died!

Mr Cluff put on an Easter-egg hunt for our last afternoon. Mat was the winner, finding *sixteen* eggs. She refused to eat them because she didn't want to get pimples when Gavin O'Donnell was coming home for the holidays, so I kindly offered to eat them for her.

Miss McKenzie ended the day with a tune on the bagpipes, while Gary and Nick did a fantastic Highland fling. We were all rapt. Nick flung himself so hard that he knocked over Gary, who then tumbled down Harry's hole to China. Miss McKenzie laughed so hard that she couldn't play the bagpipes any more (thank goodness!!!). Lynette laughed so much she wet her pants.

All in all it was a huge success.

I am writing this on the bus and hope that Dad will be home with Sophie, Peter and Xiu by the time I get to Hillrose Poo …

Good Friday, 7 April

BLISS!!!!!

Everyone is home together. Even Miss McKenzie will be here for Easter. She broke her nose again in a pig chariot race with Wes after school yesterday, just before she was due to drive off to Sydney. Fantastic!

Even better, Dad didn't get a job. He tried, but there are so many farmers looking for extra work at the moment that there just wasn't anything around. I know we really need the extra money, but I couldn't help letting out a cheer and throwing myself into Dad's arms.

Wes and Fez offered to make some money by going to work for NASA. They reckon they've nearly perfected their rocket production. Dad said he'd be happy if they'd just lay off smashing any more windows until the drought was over. Wes and Fez smiled innocently. I don't think they've given Mum and Dad the note from Mr Cluff about the school window yet.

Gerty went crazy this morning. Miss McKenzie was too sore and dizzy to get out of bed and play the bagpipes, so Gertrude paced up and down the veranda of Serenity Cottage, squealing and frothing at the mouth. Finally, she flung herself at the door, tearing it off its hinges.

Mum and Dad were really embarrassed. It was bad enough that we'd broken Miss McKenzie's nose *twice*. Now her door was demolished and she'd woken up with Gerty's fat snout snuffling in her face.

Miss McKenzie was very kind about it all. She just smiled underneath her swollen nose and said, 'Och, let her be. Where else in the world can you wake up to the magpies carolling, the cockatoos squawking and a bonnie pig smiling into your face?'

Xiu has brought a whole suitcase of firecrackers with him. He spent hours hidden away in the hayshed with Wes and Fez today, teaching them how to make rockets out of gunpowder and all the other bits and pieces you find when you pull firecrackers apart. Mum will freak when she finds out.

Sophie and I baked hot cross buns for lunch, and she helped me feed the sheep their tiny portion of drought hay this afternoon. Soon all the hay will be gone … then what?

Peter helped Dad fix fences all day.

And tonight we sat down together, all of us

around the table, and ate chicken chop suey (Mum's idea of what Xiu likes) and steamed golden syrup pudding with custard made from fresh eggs.

BLISS!!!!

Saturday, 8 April
One day until the big Easter party.

Dad, Peter and Xiu spent the morning gathering dead trees from all around the farm to make a gigantic bonfire. Sophie and I helped Mum cook a feast — casseroles, bacon and egg pies, sausage rolls, lemon meringue pies, lamingtons and sponges. Wes and Fez spent their day building rockets out of Mr Ashmore's poly pipe offcuts and Xiu's firecrackers.

Tonight Dad announced that our baths are now limited to bucket baths, except on Sundays. The tanks are really low and we just don't have the money to buy in truckloads of water. On Sundays we can share half a bath of water between us all.

Wes and Fez declared they wouldn't wash again until the drought was over, just to help out.

Easter Sunday, 9 April
I suppose that, officially, it's 10 April because it's three in the morning.

We had our big Easter bash tonight and I think you could say that, despite a few hiccups, we all had a fantastic time ... except, perhaps, for Matilda Jane the Mature.

The Simpsons, the Sweeneys, the O'Donnells, the Hartleys and Mr Cluff were all there. Miss McKenzie came a bit late. We thought it was because her nose was still throbbing, but it was actually because Gerty had bailed her up at the front door to Serenity Cottage, and wouldn't let her past until she'd played a tune on the bagpipes and fed her three packets of shortbread biscuits.

The grown-ups sat around the fire, eating and drinking and talking about the years when they'd had bumper crops and top wool prices.

Us kids played hide-and-seek in the dark, and ran around like pork chops — except for Mat, who'd worn a white dress and didn't want to get dirty. She was even wearing a gold anklet with a love heart (!!!!!) dangling from it. I think she was trying to impress Gavin O'Donnell. But Gavin was too busy having a burping contest with Davo and Peter to notice her. Poor Mat.

Just before midnight, Xiu brought out a plastic bag stuffed full of firecrackers. Wes and Fez stuck an enormous rocket (think Apollo 11) into the dirt near where Mat was standing. The plan was to finish the night with a spectacular firecracker display by Xiu, followed by a grand finale rocket launch by Wes and Fez. This one was meant to whoosh and flame like a real rocket. I'm pretty sure Mum and Dad didn't know about it.

Mum handed out sponge cake and hot chocolate, and Dad decided to make a little speech. He made some really bad jokes, cursed the drought and said some nice things about our guests being true friends through good times and bad. Dad was just starting to introduce Xiu, when a log in the bonfire crackled and threw out a shower of sparks towards Matilda Jane the Mature, and Wes and Fez's rocket. I'm not quite sure what happened next, but at least one spark landed on the fuse of the rocket — probably ricocheted off the little golden heart on Mat's anklet! The fuse sputtered and fizzed and the rocket ignited.

Peter yelled, 'Houston, we have lift-off!'

Wes and Fez screamed and threw themselves at it, but they were too late. The rocket took off into the air, sizzling and throwing out sparks. It made terrifying squealing noises as it did a complete loop-the-loop, plunged towards the ground, flew past the plastic bag containing Xiu's firecrackers, and shot back up into the sky.

Within seconds the rocket's sparks had ignited the firecrackers, which started shooting their way through the plastic bag. They burst into the sky, throwing coloured fireballs, smoke bombs, little parachuting men and showers of sparks out all over the yard. We were deafened by the squealing, banging, hissing and whooshing noises. It was the most exciting display I've ever seen — you just didn't know what was going to happen next!!!

Xiu ran off down the driveway, terrified, screaming something in Chinese with, 'Mamma mia!' thrown in every now and then.

The rocket lurched through a final wobbly loop-the-loop, then went soaring up into the branches of the gum tree near the chook house, where it got stuck. The tree burst into flames and the whole back yard lit up like it was the middle of the day.

Nobody dreamt of putting the fire out. We hardly have enough water in the tank to clean our teeth, let alone to fight a fire. Anyway, there's no grass or crop to catch fire. Bare dirt just doesn't burn.

Mat stared at the blazing gum tree, looked down at the hole in the dirt where the rocket had been and fell over backwards, landing bum-first on a lemon meringue pie.

I wonder if Gavin prefers his women with lemon meringue pie smeared all over their bum or lamingtons squished into their hair?

Mum shook her head, rolled her eyes, then offered everyone another piece of sponge cake. (No-one was going to touch the lemon meringue pie!)

Dad picked up his violin and started to play. Mr Sweeney and Mrs Hartley joined in on their guitars and everyone started to sing. We sang and laughed until an hour ago when they all went home.

Xiu was down at the front gate near the Hillrose Poo sign when Peter and Gavin found him. He wasn't going to come back until Gavin told him he had to come and see Mat with her lemon-meringue bum.

Poor Xiu …

Poor Mat …

What a fantastic night.

Monday, 10 April

Woken up this morning by an almighty crash. The burned-out gum tree had fallen on the chicken coop. The hens laid twice as many eggs as usual!

Mum was furious. She said the chooks would have to live in the old laundry until we had time to fix the coop.

Dad told Wes and Fez they'd gone a bit too far this time, but ended by saying, 'Oh, well … I s'pose it could be worse.'

We cooked toast and scrambled eggs on the glowing stump at breakfast time. Miss McKenzie came over for toast and jam and a chat.

'I just love it here,' she said in her lovely Scottish accent. 'Och! It's the best Easter I've ever had. Truly it is!'

And really, despite the drought and all, I'd have to agree.

Sophie and I spent the rest of the day lying in bed with face masks on, reading bridal magazines (Sophie) and books (me). Today's mask was egg whites and honey. My skin felt like sandpaper but it tasted great.

Wes and Fez are determined to win the greasy pig chase tomorrow at the Hardbake Plains Bush Fire Brigade's Annual Family Fun Day. They've spent the whole day searching the internet and designing a new, improved pig chariot. They've called it The Porkinator.

Tuesday, 11 April

Came home tonight with two blue ribbons, one red ribbon and a black piglet.

Sophie and I won the three-legged race by miles because the only other serious competitors were Mr and Mrs Tomlinson. Mr Tomlinson has an artificial leg, so it was a bit tricky for them. They really did have only three legs between the two of them! Miss McKenzie won the cowpat throwing competition and Mum came second in the potato-sack race.

Dad entered the Bushman's Relay, the most serious race of the day. The first team member had to roll a huge bale of hay the length of the racetrack, the second had to carry a sack of wheat, the third had to roll a tractor tyre and the last one had to push the first team member along in a wheelbarrow. Dad went in a team with Mr Sweeney and Fred and Bert Hartley. They were going really well until Mr Cluff's team lost control of their tractor tyre and it ran over Dad, Bert and their wheelbarrow. Bert broke his little finger and his wheelbarrow.

Wes and Fez spent the day talking to the greasy pig — a little, black monster. They were feeding it sausages and patty cakes and poking at it through the cage until it squealed and snapped at them.

At three o'clock, Mr Sweeney got everyone onto the racetrack in a big circle and Banjo recited his latest poem, 'Ode to the Greasy Pig Chase':

Oh, what's this in the hessian bag?
A chunky little porker.
We'll catch him and we'll roast him.
The feast will be a corker!

The bag was opened, the piglet wriggled out, the crowd roared and the greasy pig chase was on. All the little kids were diving and grabbing, but the piglet had far too much energy. He darted through the first ring of kids and started dodging the big kids and adults. For a moment it looked like he was just going to run around and around inside the circle, but then he put his blocky little head down and charged. Mr Tomlinson's artificial leg snapped at the knee joint and the greasy pig bolted down the road.

A lot of people gave up the chase once the piglet left the racetrack, but Miss McKenzie, a dozen farmers and a small group of boys raced after him. They chased him around the church, through Mrs Whittington's back yard, around the Fire Brigade shed and through the pub. Miss McKenzie and the farmers stopped at the pub for a lemon squash, and most of the boys were distracted by a big goanna, so by the time the piglet circled back to the schoolyard, next to the racetrack, only Wes, Fez and Xiu were left in the chase. Wes and Xiu got bogged up to their knees in Sam Wotherspoon's compost heap, but Fez swam on through the green sludge and disappeared under the schoolhouse after the piglet. There was some cursing and squealing followed by a couple of bumps and a loud cracking noise. A cloud of dust puffed out from between the veranda stairs, and everything fell silent.

Everyone gathered around the gateway between the racetrack and the schoolyard.

Mr Sweeney chuckled and asked Mum if she thought he needed to fetch his vet's bag. Mrs Whittington started to tell a story about a neighbour of hers who had disappeared forty-five years ago, supposedly eaten, boots and all, by a wild boar. I was just beginning to dream of Fez being slowly chewed to pieces by a black piglet, when he crawled out from beneath the stairs. He held the piglet by the tail and the piglet had his teeth clamped tightly around Fez's other wrist. Dad tied him to the back of the ute (the piglet, not Fez unfortunately), Mr Sweeney threw Fez a few sticking plasters and we all drove home feeling very satisfied with the day's events.

Wednesday, 12 April

Played Truth or Dare in the hayshed today.

We decided that the punishment for piking out would be to stand waist-deep in the dam for half an hour, no gumboots or trousers allowed.

In the past, Xiu hadn't quite got the hang of Truth or Dare. He would ask questions for Truth like, 'Who was the first man to walk on the moon?' or, 'What is the capital of Germany?' as if it was a test of our general knowledge. For Dare he'd say things like, 'I dare you to eat all your peas tonight before you eat your potato,' or, 'I dare you to wear your underpants inside out.' I mean, who would know??? Maybe it's the cultural difference or the language barrier. Last time we played, Xiu couldn't understand why Wes didn't have to eat a tablespoon of hot chillies for not telling us the height of Mount Kilimanjaro.

Anyway, today Xiu finally started to catch on to the game, and he hit the jackpot with his first Truth. He asked Fez what had made that loud cracking noise when he chased the piglet under the school.

Fez screwed up his face. He looked like he was going to pass, but he was still freaked out by the leeches in the dam. He whispered that he'd had a little accident with one of the schoolhouse stumps … He'd dived, seized the piglet in a James Bond type move, clutched it to his chest and skidded full pelt into one of the stumps. The stump snapped in two (loud cracking noise!) and the top half was left dangling from the floorboards by just a couple of nails and several hundred termites.

Fez, like the rest of us, knows that stumps are for holding a building up. Mum is still fuming mad about the chicken coop disaster, and Mr Cluff isn't likely to see the funny side of a crumbling, termite-infested schoolhouse. So Fez hadn't said a word to anyone.

Our rules for Truth or Dare say that any Truths shared during the game are never to be spoken to anyone else, otherwise you face every punishment from every single game of Truth or Dare ever played.

Our lips are sealed!

Thursday, 13 April

Sophie has been great this holiday. She still harps on about beauty and fashion, and she is considering piercing her nose, but she also comes around on the sheep run with me and does all the other farm stuff.

Wes and Fez have named their greasy pig Gunther. They are feeding him every scrap they can get their hands on. Doris and Mildred are annoyed that they have to share their food.

Miss McKenzie has decided to stay at the farm for the holidays. She's re-painting Serenity Cottage in between dizzy spells. It must be a bummer having

your nose broken twice
in three months. But with
a bit of luck the swelling
won't go down so quickly this time,
and she and I can have matching noses!

Friday, 14 April

Sophie and I spent hours this morning trying to get our hair to curl just like Miss McKenzie's. I even did some fashion designing, including a wedding dress that looks a lot like the lemon meringue pie that Mat sat on.

Mum took Wes and Fez into Dubbo today to the dentist. I don't know why she bothers. It's only a matter of time before they knock all their teeth out in some hideous accident and then all this dentist business will have been an enormous waste of money. She'd be better off spending the money on water for the tank, or hay for the sheep!

Saturday, 15 April

Dad has a job.

It doesn't start for two weeks, but when it does start it's in Sydney. We won't even get to see him on weekends. It's a factory job.

Mongrel drought.

Sunday, 16 April

I cried all night long.

Sophie heard me crying, so she got into my bed and gave me a hug.

She reminded me that it's not forever, just as long as the drought goes on.

Right now it feels like the drought will go on forever. But I couldn't say that. If I say that aloud maybe it will come true. I just started to bawl my eyes out again.

We went to church and I cried all through the service. I couldn't even raise a smile when Wes tripped over Gabby Woodhouse's baby brother's rattle and bashed his chin on the edge of the pew.

Monday, 17 April

Sophie's idea of cheering me up is to do girl stuff. It's my idea of a sure way to drag me into a deeper depression. But today, before I really knew what I was doing, I was lying alongside Mum, Miss McKenzie and Sophie on a quilt under a kurrajong tree, in my cossies, with cucumber slices on my eyes and a mask of rolled oats and honey smeared all over my face and neck.

'The cucumber is to take the puff out of your eyes and the oatmeal and honey is to cleanse and moisturise your skin,' Sophie told us in her best beautician's voice.

Miss McKenzie laughed and said, 'Och! Don't I need cucumber on my poor nose more than my eyes?'

Actually, it turns out that the cucumber was an entrée and the oatmeal and honey was the main course ...

We were just getting really relaxed when I heard a snuffle in my ear. Gerty hoovered both slices of cucumber from my eyes and began licking the honey and oatmeal from my face and neck with her fat, slimy tongue. At the same time Doris and Mildred were making a quick meal out of Mum's and Miss McKenzie's face masks.

Sophie jumped up screaming and ran towards the house but Mildred and Doris, who are extremely fit from their chariot racing, soon outran her. Doris knocked Sophie off her feet and Mildred licked every last speck of oatmeal from her face. Gunther appeared from nowhere and bit a hole in the back of Sophie's bikini pants.

I laughed so much that my tummy ached. It was the best beauty treatment I've ever had. It really did cheer me up!

Tuesday, 18 April

Dad must be feeling pretty bad about having to work away from home. Today he spent three hours in the machinery shed with Wes, Fez, Peter and Xiu, making fuel-powered rockets out of Xiu's firecrackers!

Mum must be feeling pretty bad about the firecrackers because this evening she spent three hours on the lounge with an oatmeal mask on her face and cucumber slices on her eyes.

Wednesday, 19 April

Gunther is only three months old and he is already a monster!

Today Wes was giving Fluffles his cereal bowl to lick the leftover milk out of, when Gunther sneaked up behind him and bit him on the leg. And then he wouldn't let go!

Doris is pretty mean to Wes at times, but she

came to the rescue and bit Gunther on *his* leg. And she wouldn't let go!

By the time Dad came to the rescue, Wes's pyjama pants were in shreds, Gunther had a huge gash in his back leg and Wes had to be driven to the Sweeneys' for five stitches.

Thursday, 20 April

Spent the day with Sophie and Miss McKenzie, painting Serenity Cottage. Actually, we spent half the day painting and the other half watching old movies and eating popcorn.

Miss McKenzie is like a big sister, only better. She's all the fun and she's past all the fluff and frenzy over boys and clothes and make-up. Sometimes I think she's like a grown-up me … except for the bagpipes.

Friday, 21 April

Peter had to break up a fight today between Gunther and two of the dogs. I think the dogs came out second best!

Mrs Sweeney, Mat and Lynette came over for lunch.

Mat and Sophie spent hours braiding each other's hair and talking about how absolutely fabulous body piercing looks. It would have been a total waste of a day except that it ended with Sophie talking Mat into letting her pierce her bellybutton. Lynette tried to run out of the room to tell Mrs Sweeney, but I grabbed her, shoved her onto my bed and sat on her. This had every chance of being as entertaining as the facial treatment we had on Monday.

Sophie told Mat to lie down on her bed and pull her shirt up. She grabbed Mum's sewing kit and pulled out the biggest needle she could find.

Mat turned deathly white.

'Sure you want to do this?' Sophie asked.

Mat looked like she was going to say no, but Sophie really wanted to try this out, and preferably on someone other than herself, so she said, 'Gavin reckons pierced bellybuttons are drop-dead gorgeous.'

That was it! Clever Sophie. Mat shut her eyes tightly, clenched her fists by her side and said, 'Do it!'

So Sophie did it.

I thought Mat would be a wimp, but obviously her love for Gavin O'Donnell is greater than the pain of having a needle stuck through her belly and a safety pin threaded through the hole afterwards. I was really hoping for a full faint, or at least a blood-curdling scream. But Mat gave nothing. I can't help respecting her for that.

And just think, if ever the elastic goes in her undies she will always have a safety pin to mend them. That's got to be handy.

Saturday, 22 April

Bummer.

Here we go again.

Sophie, Peter and Xiu go back to boarding school tomorrow.

Mum and I are driving them over to Bathurst this time, and we'll get to have afternoon tea at the school with all the other families who are throwing their children out of home for the term. Mum said it would be a good chance for me to have a look around and get familiar with the place, ready for next year. I tried to throw her a withering stare like the ones Mat gives me, but I just ended up bursting into tears.

Started reading Lemony Snicket's *A Series of Unfortunate Events*. I thought Klaus, Violet and

Sunny's problems might make mine seem a bit smaller by comparison.

So far it's not working ...

Sunday, 23 April

They're gone. Sophie and Peter are gone.

And this time next week Dad will be gone.

Mat is gone. Matilda Jane the Mature has totally swallowed her up.

Hundreds of the sheep are gone ... dead.

Half of Mum is gone, she's getting so skinny.

One more dust storm and the farm will be gone.

All I'll have left is Wes and Fez.

Bummer.

Had a look around the boarding school with Sophie and her best friend, Anna. I tried to check out every possible escape route, but got a bit distracted when they took me down to the farm plot. They've got twelve different crop and vegetable trials running, as well as chickens and three *beautiful* Black Angus calves. Apparently you can study Agriculture from year seven on! They also have real grass tennis courts and a footy oval FOR THE GIRLS! How cool is that?

Not that I want to go to boarding school or

anything, but it's good to know that the girls who *do* stick with it learn more than how to apply the perfect coat of nail polish and how to pierce their bellybuttons without getting blood on their school blazers!

Talking about bellybuttons, Lynette ratted on Mat, Sophie and me. Don't know why *I* got into trouble. It was Sophie who did the piercing, it was Mat's bellybutton, and if we're going to get technical, it was *Mum's* needle! I pointed this out to Mum but she didn't see the funny side.

Monday, 24 April

HOORAY!!!!

I can't believe it!

Just as the bus arrived at the school this morning, a semitrailer pulled out of the gate, LEAVING AN ENO-R-R-R-MOUS STACK OF HAY BALES BEHIND.

It looked like a mountain of gold had fallen into the playground. It was like finding an oasis in the desert … like waking up and finding your slippers full of diamonds.

I know a pile of hay is not most kids' idea of a thrill, but everyone at school was busting with excitement. Hay is precious … and expensive!

Ned Murphy kept shouting, 'But how did it get here? How did it get here?'

Lynette reckoned it must have been a mistake, like a mix-up with the mail or with the luggage on a train.

Nick pulled a piece of hay off one of the bales and rolled it between his fingers. He handed some to Jack who chewed it, nodded and said it was tip-top quality.

Mr Cluff ran out of the classroom, smiling and waving a big white envelope with golden edges. When he handed it to *me*, I began to shake.

Everyone was dead silent as I read it aloud.

My most esteemed friend Blue,

I hope your cold sore is better. There is nothing to be ashamed of in having a wide nose. Here in Brughistan we say that a large nose is a symbol of great intelligence, beauty and wisdom. At least that is what *I* say, because my nose is as big as the pyramids of Egypt!

I am hoping that fifty truckloads of hay will be of some help to you and your farmer friends. They should all arrive within a few weeks of each other. Please let me know if you need more.

My horses hope your sheep enjoy their food. I truly hope your father does not need to shoot any more sheep.

Please don't forget the recipe for the steamed golden syrup pudding. My head chef is anxious to make it. My wife does not cook. I have bought 200 new chickens to ensure a steady supply of fresh eggs for the custard.

Yours sincerely,

The Sultan of Brughistan

(But you can call me Brue. Get it? Blue and Brue. We sound like a pop band!)

We should have been starting our lessons but Mr Cluff ran into the office to ring our families with the news.

Miss McKenzie broke out the bagpipes and we did a celebratory Highland fling. We leapt and

danced around the mountain of gold, singing and cheering like lunatics, until the wind picked up and the dust drove us inside.

Tuesday, 25 April, Anzac Day

Wrote Brue a letter this morning and posted it when we went into town for the Anzac Day service. Here's what I wrote:

Dear Brue,

Thank you! Thank you! Thank you! A million times thank you for the beautiful, golden hay you have sent us. You are my favourite oil tycoon in the whole wide world.

Thanks to your hay there are thousands of grateful sheep chewing more food tonight than they have eaten in ages. There are also more farmers with hope that they might make it through the drought.

But best of all, thanks to your hay, my dad can wait for at least another month before he leaves home to work in Sydney. The money we will save on the next truckload of hay can be used to buy some water for the tanks and maybe pay one or two bills.

If you were here at Hardbake Plains I would give you a hundred kisses on your enormous nose and I would bake you a steamed golden syrup pudding myself. But for now you will just have to accept the recipe, which I have enclosed.

THANK YOU! YOU ARE A LIFE SAVER!!!!!

Your best friend, and fellow big nose,

Blue xxxxxxx

Wednesday, 26 April

Harry Wilson's getting really serious about his project. He honestly believes that he can dig to China by Christmas time. Actually, he's decided that he wants to get there by the first of December, so he has time to do his Christmas shopping in Beijing and still be home in time for the Christmas picnic on the last day of school.

During the holidays, Harry watched this old war movie called *The Great Escape*, where prisoners of war were tunnelling out of a prison camp. It's a true story. They had to get rid of all the dirt from the tunnel without the prison guards realising what they were doing, so they made bags to wear under their trousers. They filled the bags with the dirt and slowly let it out as they walked around the prison yard each day, trampling the dirt into the ground without anyone noticing.

Harry got his mum to make him a pair of those bags for under his trousers. Now he spends any time that he isn't digging to China, walking around the playground with a fine trail of dirt pouring out behind him. He's unloading an amazing amount of soil.

Gunther bit the tip off Fluffles' tail this afternoon. That pig is out of control.

Thursday, 27 April

Mat wasn't at school today.

Her bellybutton is infected.

Friday, 28 April

Scary news. Three criminals who escaped from a high-security prison in Sydney two days ago have headed out west. The local news said a truck driver from Dubbo reckoned he'd given them a lift out our way, but couldn't be sure. He didn't realise they were crooks when he picked them up, of course.

Wes and Fez have tied Gunther up to the veranda post outside their bedroom window for the night.

'Guard pigs are better than guard dogs,' Wes explained.

In Gunther's case I think they might be right.

Saturday, 29 April

Mum, Miss McKenzie and I went into town today for the CWA's Autumn Cake Festival. I won Best Chocolate Cake and Mum won Best Overall Cook for her orange fruit cake, ginger fluff sponge and lemon meringue pie (and, no, Mat didn't sit in it — ha, ha, ha!).

Mrs Whittington came over to congratulate me and got a bit confused. She said, 'Lovely essay, Blue. The bush is the heart of our country. Well done, darling. Well done. I'll bring you a steamed golden syrup pudding to school on Monday morning.'

I was going to mention that I won the prize for my *chocolate cake* but Miss McKenzie squeezed my shoulder and said, 'Och, won't that be a treat, Blue? We'll look forward to seeing you on Monday, Mrs W.'

When we got home, Dad had Gunther's head wedged between two bales of hay so that he couldn't bite him while his tail was being bandaged.

'Rocket burns,' Dad explained.

I think he was about to say, 'It could be worse,' but Mum threw him a dirty look, walked inside and lay on the lounge with two slices of cucumber over her eyes.

Sunday, 30 April

Dad has just been bandaging Fez's bum.

Wes and Fez are determined to break Mr Cluff's thirty-five second record on Davo and Jack's BMX track at school. They reckoned a rocket-powered bike should do the trick. So today they made a monster rocket with firecrackers and an old tennis ball tin and tied it to the back of Peter's bike just under the seat.

What more can I say? Fez sits, Wes lights, rocket fires, seat catches on fire, pants catch fire, bum burns, Dad bandages bum.

 I'm still not sure what happened to Gunther's tail ...

May

Monday, 1 May

Steamed golden syrup pudding for lunch again.

Mrs Whittington was a bit upset today. She kept going on about three of her chooks being stolen. Mr Cluff said that maybe it was a fox, but Mrs Whittington kept saying they were stolen.

Miss McKenzie had to take her home and make her a cup of tea to calm her down, even though it was the middle of class.

Harry Wilson has unloaded so much dirt in the playground that little mounds have started to appear everywhere. I don't suppose it matters that much, except on the soccer field. Today I was dribbling happily along when something like an ant hill rose up and tripped me over just three metres from the goal. Very disappointing.

Harry still won't let anyone in his hole, even though it's big enough to hide an elephant in. He's worried that he might be just millimetres from China and the intruder will be the first to break through. He doesn't want to do all that hard work just so someone else can take the glory.

Tuesday, 2 May

Banjo showed me something *really* cool today.

Mr Cluff was droning on about rainforest plants and I totally lost interest. It's a bit hard to relate to forests so damp that mould grows on animals' fur and mushrooms sprout overnight. I mean, it's so dry here at the moment that if you sit outside with a glass of water a whole flock of sparrows will land on you and start fighting over who's going to bath in it first! That's if the wild ducks don't beat them to it ...

Anyway, Banjo saw me rolling my eyes and winked at me. He leant down beneath his desk, pulled a flap of carpet back and lifted up a short section of floorboard. Sitting in a little alcove beneath the floor was his latest notepad and his favourite pencil. He lifted them out, put the floorboard and carpet back in place, and looked Mr Cluff square in the eye just in time to answer a question about aerial roots. Then, once he'd given an intelligent answer and Mr Cluff directed his attention to someone else, Banjo started to work on his latest poem, 'Ode to My Cat's Mange Problem'.

Genius!

Later, Banjo said I could put my diary there if I liked, but I had to be sure not to give the hiding spot away. I'll take it to school tomorrow. It might come in handy because we're starting fractions and decimals next week. Urk!

Mrs Whittington was over at school again this afternoon, telling Miss McKenzie and Mr Cluff that not only were her chooks being stolen, but food and blankets were going missing too.

They didn't really take her seriously because Mrs Whittington is *always* losing things. Just before Easter she was certain that her birdbath had been stolen. Miss McKenzie found it standing in the middle of the kitchen, full of fruit. The fruit bowl was out in the garden, full of water, with willy wagtails bathing in it.

Wednesday, 3 May

I couldn't get to sleep last night. What if those three escaped prisoners are at Hardbake Plains? What if it was them, not a fox that stole Mrs Whittington's chooks? Or they could be hiding on our farm! What if they steal our chooks? What if they kidnap Miss McKenzie from Serenity Cottage? What if they have guns???

When I finally did fall asleep, I had a horrible dream. The baddies killed Mum, Dad and me and plastered us up in the mud walls with all the other bones while Gunther stood outside the window and laughed. Miss McKenzie screamed for them to stop and threw chocolate at them, but they punched her in the face and broke her nose. Wes and Fez escaped in their chariots.

I am writing this at school in the middle of a maths lesson. Mr Cluff just asked me something about rounding off 9.6738 to three decimal points and I stared at him stupidly. He said not to worry because most kids found decimals tricky at first and I would catch on.

Not if I don't listen …

Thursday, 4 May

Dad was in collecting a load of hay after school today when Mrs Whittington came running across the road in her pyjamas, two beanies and a pearl necklace, crying.

Bob, her rotten, ugly, selfish son, is on the warpath again. He wants her back in that nursing home once and for all. He said all this nonsense about stolen chooks and missing blankets just proves that she can't look after herself. He's bringing a doctor and a lawyer tomorrow to declare her unfit to live alone.

Dad sat Mrs W down on a bale of hay and called Miss McKenzie. Miss McKenzie made her a nice cup of tea and calmed her down a bit. I gave her the custard tart from my lunch that I'd been saving for the ride home. I'd do anything for Mrs Whittington.

When Miss McKenzie suggested that Mrs Whittington's son might be a wee bit selfish, Mrs Whittington yelled, 'He's a back-stabbing, stingy, nasty beast! I'm ashamed to call him my son. I'd be ashamed to even call him my dog, because it'd be an insult to mutts and mangy mongrels all over the world!'

She sure was upset.

Dad went inside and rang Bob Whittington, three different doctors and the nursing home. They all agreed that the only way Mrs Whittington could stay in her home was if she had someone living with her.

Mrs Whittington sobbed. She said she'd die if they took her back there. They'd take her spirit away and she'd be nothing but a hollow shell. She'd rather they put her down like a sick cow.

I couldn't stand it. I love Mrs Whittington, not to mention her steamed golden syrup puddings.

Miss McKenzie's bottom lip began to wobble and I thought she was going to cry too. But all of a sudden she started to rave on like a lunatic.

'Och! Aren't I sick to death of all that travelling to and from Hillrose Poo every day? … Must start looking for a place to live in Hardbake Plains … blah, blah, blah … What about that lovely little sleep-out at the back of your house, Mrs W? … I *love* pumpkin soup and I know you make the best in town, Mrs W … blabber, blabber, blabber … No, of course I don't mind having purple and lime green curtains in my bedroom …'

I held my breath in horror at what I knew she would say next.

'Lovely! I'll move in on Saturday.'

Just like that!

Miss McKenzie has saved Mrs Whittington from the clutches of Bob the back-stabbing, mangy mongrel and the Autumn Meadows Nursing Home. I think she's wonderful for doing such a kind and generous thing.

But losing her freckly nose and smiley face from Hillrose Poo …

I threw myself into Dad's ute and slammed the door. Snot snorted down my face and I burst into tears.

Friday, 5 May

I'm writing this in class again! Diary writing seems more exciting when you have to do it in secret.

Spent lunch time under the schoolhouse with Banjo. I couldn't bear to play soccer with Miss McKenzie in case I started to cry. Besides, the soccer field is getting so lumpy with Harry's soil that it's impossible to dribble the ball in a straight line.

Banjo said I should try to put my sadness into a poem. He said it didn't even have to rhyme. It just needed to show my true feelings. This is what I came up with:

> My guts are torn out
> A little bit more
> With every person who leaves.
> Peter.
> Sophie.
> Miss McKenzie, don't go.
> I am bleeding to death.
> Soon I will be
> DEAD.

I showed Banjo and he nodded thoughtfully.
He said, 'I think you should play more soccer.'

Saturday, 6 May

I didn't think anyone could be more miserable than me.

But that was before I saw how bad Gerty was. Poor pig.

Her day started like any other day. She listened to the bagpipes, gobbled a bickie and snuffled Miss McKenzie's leg as she climbed into her car.

But when the sun set and there was no sign of Miss McKenzie returning, Gerty got restless. She trotted up and down the veranda of Serenity Cottage, getting faster and faster each time. Every three or four laps she jumped up, put her front trotters on the window sill and squealed like a demon-possessed witch. She was frothing at the mouth and the hairs along her back stood up straight as lightning rods.

By eight-thirty she'd started throwing herself at the front door. Dad had reinforced the hinges since her last break-in, but she threw herself at it again and again until the door splintered into hundreds of tiny pieces. She charged through the cottage, squealing and snorting from room to room, tearing curtains and knocking furniture over as she went. When she finally realised that neither the bagpipes nor Miss McKenzie were there, she dropped herself in a sulking blob onto the bathroom floor.

She's still there, snuffling and spilling huge tears.

What a devastating thing to see.

Sunday, 7 May

I had another nightmare last night …

Three escaped prisoners chased me around the farm until I ran into the house and slammed the door. They couldn't get in, so they flung themselves against the door again and again, oinking and frothing at the mouth, until it splintered into thousands of tiny pieces.

'Give us the bagpipes!' they yelled as they plastered me up in the mud walls. Gerty came in and I begged her to help, but she just cried chocolate tears and let out a moan that sounded like 'Scotland the Brave' on the bagpipes.

I woke up screaming, 'Miss McKenzie! Miss McKenzie!'

Mum came in and stroked my hair and said Gerty would be fine in the morning.

But she wasn't.

I tried to feed her some chocolate cake and porridge for breakfast, but she refused to eat, and Gerty's not the sort of pig to turn down food.

I thought a tune on the recorder might cheer her up, but it didn't. She got quite agitated and chased me into the garden. I think she would have bitten me if I hadn't shoved the recorder up her nostril.

Mum said Gerty'd be right in the evening.

But she wasn't.

When we got home from tennis at the Simpsons', there was no sign of Gertrude.

We drove round and round the farm until dark, but we couldn't find her.

It's ten o'clock now and she still isn't home.

Maybe she'll be back in the morning.

Monday, 8 May

Gerty's not back.

It's eight o'clock in the evening and there's still no sign of her. She'll be starving hungry and lonely and scared, and she's probably going through terrible withdrawal symptoms after three whole days without the bagpipes.

I rang Sophie tonight and begged her to come home and help me find Gerty, but she said she has a science exam tomorrow and doesn't want to miss the dance with the boys' school on Thursday night. I suppose boys are more important to her than Gerty.

I find that VERY DISAPPOINTING.

Tuesday, 9 May

Good old Brue!

Another truckload of hay has been delivered to the school over the weekend. This load looks even better than the last.

I wish Brue lived at the Bake. He'd know what to do about Gerty and Miss McKenzie and Matilda Jane the Mature and the terrible twins.

Wednesday, 10 May

9.40 am

I'm a hostage!

All of us at Hardbake Plains Public School are hostages in our own classroom — Miss McKenzie, Mr Cluff and seventeen kids.

There should be nineteen kids, but Wes and Fez are WAGGING!!!! They sneaked off somewhere down behind Mr Jackson's shearing shed when the bus arrived at school. They had a big bag of poly pipes, matches, string, firecrackers and cereal and were whispering something about the Mother Of All Rockets.

Maybe Wes and Fez will rescue us!

WHO AM I TRYING TO KID?????

Anyway, Banjo and I agree that it's our duty to record everything that goes on. It might come in handy in court … or at our funerals … Besides, it helps to keep me calm …

This is what's happened so far …

This morning we all jogged into the state forest to train for the cross-country run at Allantown. Miss McKenzie was in the lead, Mr Cluff at the rear.

Halfway round the track Lucy Ferris let out a blood-curdling scream.

I thought she must have found something really gross like a dead wombat or a maggot-infested kangaroo but what she'd found was three very big, dirty, nasty-looking men. I nearly fainted when I saw the gun that one of them had pointed at Lucy's back.

Miss McKenzie hustled the little kids along behind Lucy and the man with the gun. She was trying to sound cheerful and chatty to keep the little kids calm but her voice sounded strange and squeaky.

The second bloke, who Banjo and I have christened Gorilla Dude, shoved Mr Cluff in the back, and said a few very nasty words. The third bloke, hereby known as Veranda Head (very big forehead but not filled with brains, I suspect), walked behind us all, snarling and jabbing Ben Simpson in the back. Poor Ben cried all the way back to school.

I kept hoping and praying that someone would spot us and come to the rescue, but no-one goes into the bush much.

For once in my life, I hate that Hardbake Plains is such a quiet little town.

10.45 am

Phew! Gorilla Dude is dumb!!!

He got suspicious of all my writing and grabbed my diary. I told him it's my science book and I'm writing an essay on rainforests. I pointed to all the posters of ferns and sloths and jungles around the classroom and he tossed my diary back!!!! The picture is to prove my point!

Doofus!

Hope he's too dumb to think of killing off his hostages ...

11.08 am
Nick Farrel keeps grinning stupidly and saying, 'So this is what it's like to be a hostage.'

He seems to think being kidnapped is cool!!!

He keeps staring at the bloke with the gun. Gunman seems a bit uneasy. Maybe he thinks Nick's getting a good look at him so that he can identify him to the police later on. He needn't worry. Nick can't even remember his two-times tables most of the time.

At eleven o'clock Tom Gillies asked if he should ring the bell for recess!!!

I wish!

11.47 pm
We're all thirsty and hungry and the three kindergarten kids are busting to go to the loo.

Miss McKenzie has now read twenty-seven picture books to the junior class. Veranda Head laughed so much during *Green Eggs and Ham* that I thought he was going to wet his pants. He made Miss McKenzie read it four times!!!

Lynette Sweeney *has* just wet her pants.

12.09 pm

Gorilla Dude, Veranda Head and Gunman have raided our lunchboxes and scoffed all our food! They must be really hungry after living out in the bush for weeks.

Grace Simpson, who has a huge appetite, was positively starving after missing out on play lunch and got really cross. She sneaked a few dominoes into a cheese sandwich and Veranda Head cracked his tooth. Now he's spitting chips! Or should I say he's spitting dominoes and bits of broken tooth?

Sam can't bear to see all that food disappearing. Right now he's hovering around Gunman with his compost bucket, waiting for him to finish a banana.

'You won't throw that peel in the bin, will ya? They make great compost, banana skins, ya know. They rot down to a lovely brown gunge. The zucchinis thrive on 'em — unless ya put too much on and then ya suffocate 'em, which is what I did last time. But I'll try again in the spring and maybe this time I'll get a Guinness World Record for the biggest zucchini.'

Sam's already pestered Gorilla Man so much that he handed his scraps over just to shut him up.

12.50 pm

Gabby Woodhouse has just suggested a bit of hairdressing to our kidnappers!!!

She told them their hair was a disgrace and they'd never get past the police like that because they *looked* like criminals, didn't they? Then she offered to give them haircuts for two dollars a piece!!!

Veranda Head roared. Gorilla Dude snatched the scissors from Gabby's hand and shoved her onto the mat.

Gabby wasn't even scared. She was just cheesed off.

She yelled, 'Just because I gave Lynette a crew cut, no-one trusts me any more!'

Some of the kids just don't seem to realise what a serious situation we're in.

Jack and Davo, for instance, have been quizzing our kidnappers about all the snakes in the bush.

'Seen any taipans out there?'

'How about black snakes? Gotta love black snakes!'

'Those brown fellas can get pretty big.'

'Have you heard about the Silent Killers? You know those snakes that bite you, but you don't even know you've been bitten until you swell up like a balloon and drop down dead. It can take days to die. Reckon it'd just about be the worst way to go! The bush around here is teemin' with 'em.'

That seemed to freak Gorilla Dude out something fierce.

1.18 pm

Gary and Nick are rapt in Veranda Head's tattoos. His shirt is torn and you can see a different tattoo through every hole.

Gary keeps asking if he's got any dragons.

Nick wants to know if he's got any tattoos on his bum. Apparently Nick's Great Uncle Winston's got a slice of pizza tattooed on his bum. Nick's Great Aunty Loretta's Italian. They met during the war. And that's meant to explain the pizza tattoo???

They're driving Veranda Head insane, which wouldn't be a bad thing except that they're driving the rest of us insane too!

1.40 pm

Good grief! As if we haven't got enough to deal with, Matilda Jane the Mature is at it again.

She has spent most of the day filing her nails and giving our kidnappers her best withering stares. They are too dumb to notice.

Now she's talking drivel.

'Now if these men had been to *boarding school*, none of this would be happening right now.'

'No-one from *boarding school* would ever commit a crime.'

'*Boarding school* teaches people the correct way to behave.'

1.50 pm

I just tipped Sam's bucketload of compost over Mat's head.

Very satisfying.

Mat's crying. Sultanas and yoghurt are dripping down her face as I write.

Sam is going ballistic about it being a tragic waste of good compost.

Lynette laughed so much that she has just wet her pants again.

And I think ... YES!!!!

Mrs Whittington has just wandered in, wearing her wedding dress and gumboots, carrying a piping hot steamed golden syrup pudding ...

2.12 pm

Missed out on the pudding, but I got a pile of pork!

158

Ha! Ha! Ha!

Mrs W arrived, saying the usual: 'Ah, Blue. There you are, darling. I've finally made that pudding I promised you. Lovely essay, darling. The bush is the heart of our beautiful country. Well done. Well done. Enjoy the pudding.'

She'd only just said 'pudding', when my beloved Gerty tore through the screen door into the classroom, knocked Gunman backwards into a crate of blocks and bolted towards the pudding. She head-butted it out of Mrs W's hands and onto the floor, where she gobbled it all up and licked the carpet clean. She must have been starving after walking thirty kilometres to town and not eating for four days!

I was so excited to see Gerty, I rushed to hug her.

Mrs W said, 'That's a mighty big sheepdog you've got there, young Blue.'

Then she stared at our kidnappers and said, 'I don't suppose you chappies have come across those three prisoners who are meant to be lurking around in the bush? They've stolen my chickens, you know. I'll give them a good spanking if I ever get my hands on them.'

Miss McKenzie burst out laughing.

Verandah Head banged his head against the whiteboard, Gorilla Dude's eyes rolled back in his head and I swear I saw Gunman's bottom lip begin to wobble.

I think the crims are starting to think they've bitten off more than they can chew.

2.33 pm

Mr Cluff asked our kidnappers to let all the children go and just keep the adults hostage. They told him to SIDDOWN AND SHUDDUP!!!!!!!!!

Harry Wilson kicked Gunman in the shin!!!!

I don't think they really know what they're going to do with us. I suppose we just ran into them in the bush, so they had to take us hostage. They couldn't possibly kill us all ... could they?

Gerty is at my feet, chewing happily on the carpet as I scratch her back with my feet. It's comforting to have her here with me.

It's getting cloudy and windy. Think we're in for another dust storm.

2.48 pm

All of our lovely hay from Brue is on fire and it's all Wes and Fez's fault!

160

I'm writing this face down on the floor and it's *not easy*, but Banjo says we must record *everything*. I don't see *him* doing much writing. He's been stuck on finding a word that rhymes with 'hostages' since 10 am!!!

A few minutes ago, a high-pitched whistling noise cut through the air followed by hundreds of loud bangs like machine-gun fire. Everyone ran to the windows just in time to witness the Mother Of All Rockets flying and jerking (mostly jerking!) through the air. It was huge! It was throwing out fireballs, exploding penny bungers and what looked like whole Catherine wheels. I think I even saw cereal raining down from its jet stream. The rocket broke into loop-the-loops, got caught up in a gust of wind and torpedoed towards the school, where it crashed into the Sultan of Brughistan's hay with a phenomenal explosion! The hay burst into flames, the wind whipped the fire into an inferno and the fire siren began wailing from down the road.

Gunman waved his gun and roared at us, 'Lie down on the floor and stay there!!!!'

Well, that's not *exactly* what he said. His version had some extremely bad words scattered through it.

Now Grace Simpson and Sarah Love are crying.

Ned Murphy is snoring!

Before I left the window, I caught a glimpse of Wes and Fez running towards the schoolyard, yelling and cheering.

So much for them coming to our rescue!!!

3.36 pm

I'm starving and busting to go to the loo and it's getting *really* crowded in here.

The siren brought the Bush Fire Brigade members rushing in from nearby farms, the CWA women arrived with refreshments and first-aid kits, and the fire truck came blaring down the road, and into the schoolyard.

We could hear men shouting, water gushing, rakes and shovels belting at the hay and Betty Simpson shouting out her pumpkin sultana cake recipe to Mrs Flanagan.

Finally, we heard Trevor McMahon give the all clear and heavy boots stomped up onto the veranda.

Gorilla Dude began to weep, 'No more. Please, no more.'

It didn't help. The whole Bush Fire Brigade

and CWA charged in, shovels, sponge cakes and all, to see if we were okay.

Mr O'Donnell asked if it was nap time when he saw us all face down on the floor.

Gunman stepped out from behind the door and waved the twelve firemen and seven CWA women into the classroom with his gun.

It's getting uncomfortably crowded in here and the building is starting to make weird groaning noises under the weight of all these extra people.

The crooks are really edgy. Gunman keeps pointing his gun at us, screaming and swearing. No-one is game to talk any more.

4.05 pm

I really don't think they've thought this hostage thing through properly. We should all be on the school bus by now and when we don't arrive home our parents will come looking for us. There's no way an extra thirty people will fit in here. The floorboards are groaning enough as it is.

Mr Macintosh waited out the front for all the bus kids for about ten minutes, then wandered in whistling 'The Wheels on the Bus Go Round and Round'.

Veranda Head cried, 'Now this *has* to be all of 'em!'

Then Mr Sweeney charged in with his vet's bag, yelling, 'Anyone hurt in the fire? I was just about to tranquillize Pete Scott's horse, when I heard that the fire brigade had been called out ...'

His voice faded as he noticed Gunman. He pulled his fist back ready to throw a punch, but suddenly let his arm drop down by his side. You can't argue with a gun.

4.40 pm

The phone keeps ringing. Our mums and dads must be wondering where we are.

There's a monster storm brewing out there. The wind is howling and tearing branches off the trees. Lightning is flashing in the distance, but it's getting harder to see because the sky is filling with thick dust.

Some of the little kids have fallen asleep from exhaustion.

I'm scared.

Davo tried to strike up another conversation about snakes, but Veranda Head gave a growl that even Davo couldn't ignore.

164

Mr Sweeney and Mr Murphy are passing eye signals over Mr Sweeney's vet's bag. Maybe he has a sandwich or some biscuits in there that he wants to sneak out. Man, I'm hungry!!

11.50 pm

Mum told me to go to sleep, but who can sleep after their mother has fed them four mugs of hot chocolate and five lamingtons?

Wes and Fez grizzled because they had to go to bed at ten o'clock after only one mug of hot chocolate. But, as Mum pointed out, *their* day was pretty much like any other day — they did something very naughty (wagged school), made something very dangerous (Mother Of All Rockets), destroyed something very precious (Brue's hay) and injured themselves (I'll get to that in a minute).

Anyway, I have to finish my record of the day's events or Banjo will *never* let me hear the end of it.

After Mr Sweeney arrived at school, two of the little kids wet their pants, Mat vomited, Mrs Whittington started lecturing Gertrude on the benefits of moisturising morning and night, and Sarah Love started screaming hysterically every time she heard a clap of thunder, which was every few seconds once the storm really got going.

Miss McKenzie's sense of humour failed her for the first time *ever* and she screamed, 'Och! You can't keep us all here forever! At least let the wee ones go. They don't deserve this!'

Veranda Head roared, 'SHUT UP!!!' and at the same instant the lights flickered and died. Talk about creepy.

The building shook violently in a sudden blast of wind. Lightning flashed, a huge clap of thunder rattled the windowpanes and Sarah let out another blood-curdling scream.

And then … joy of joys … IT STARTED TO RAIN.

And not just little pitter-patters.

Big, fat, delicious dollops of water!

The thunder rumbled on and on, but we could still hear the rain belting down through it all. It was as if the weather knew it had three years of drought to make up for. We all cheered when the gutters started to overflow.

Water began to rush in torrents across the scorched paddocks. The dry creek bed swelled up until it became a raging river and water gushed across the back of the schoolyard, washing Sam's mountain of compost down Harry Wilson's hole to China.

Meanwhile, above the rain and thunder and overflowing gutters, we heard the familiar sound of bleating sheep escaping from Mr Jackson's farm.

The sky lit up with a spectacular display of lightning, and thunder cracked like it was splitting the plains in two.

Hundreds of Mr Jackson's frightened sheep bolted for shelter under the schoolhouse, barging against the termite-infested stumps, which were already straining under the weight of all those people inside the school. Every last stump snapped in two and the schoolhouse collapsed into a sea of mud, sheep and termites.

Inside the classroom, we lurched on top of each other as the floor fell from beneath us. Tables toppled, chairs skidded across the room and blocks, atlases and crayons went flying everywhere.

Lynette shrieked as her papier-mâché solar system was crushed under a pile of dictionaries. Sam let out a cry of horror as his compost bucket was crushed under Mrs Flanagan.

Gerty landed with a belly-flop on top of Veranda Head, winding him so that he couldn't breathe, let alone move. The whiteboard fell off the wall and landed on Gerty.

Mr Sweeney grabbed a needle from his vet's bag and jabbed it into Gorilla Dude's bum, dosing him up with enough horse tranquillizer to keep him sleeping for a month.

Gunman tried to make a dash for it, but tripped over my huge feet! His gun slid across the floor, down through a crack in the floorboards and disappeared beneath the mud. He tried to get up and run but Miss McKenzie jumped in front of him.

She yelled, 'Oh no you don't! You can't scare my poor, wee children half to death and then slip away like a weasel!' and punched him in the nose. His nose broke with a sickening crunch and he fell, unconscious, to the floor. It sure must have felt good breaking someone else's nose for a change!

Mr Cluff untangled Gabby, Harry and Mrs Simpson from a pile of chairs and backpacks that was clogging the doorway and led the way outside to freedom.

Fred and Bert Hartley carried Mrs Whittington out on an upturned computer desk. She waved and nodded cheerily to us all as if she'd been crowned Miss Wool and Wheat once again.

Miss McKenzie and the Bush Fire Brigade members formed a chain to pass the little kids out over the splintered floorboards and mud, and the rest of us followed out into the rain.

Every single Hardbaker put their face up to the sky and let the raindrops flood down their cheeks and necks.

I opened my mouth and let the rain fall in.

Nothing has ever tasted better. Not even steamed golden syrup pudding!

One by one, the grown-ups began to shout and cheer, and soon nearly everyone was laughing.

Mrs Flanagan and Mr Sweeney cried.

Mr Cluff put his arm around Miss McKenzie's shoulder, gave her a squeeze and said, 'Well done, Katherine.'

We were all hugging and slapping each other on the back when, suddenly, Veranda Head scrambled from the schoolhouse wreckage, desperate to escape from Gertrude. Gerty let out a hideous squeal, dived from the rubble and chased Veranda Head across the yard. He leapt over Lucy's rabbit hutch, stumbled across Jack and Davo's BMX track, tripped over Sarah and Lynette's mud bricks and fell straight into Harry's hole to China, sinking up to his neck in Sam's compost. He couldn't escape. It must have been like drowning in quicksand, only much smellier.

Wes and Fez crept out from behind the toilet block. They gaped in disbelief at the charred remains of the haystack, the crumpled schoolhouse, the muddy sheep running in all directions, Veranda Head drowning in compost and the unconscious bodies of Gunman and Gorilla Dude being carried out of the rubble.

Not wanting to miss out on the action, they began to run across the schoolyard but got caught up in another flood of water that gushed across the paddocks. They got washed past us all towards the schoolhouse wreckage, where they collided with a floating door. Wes — black eye. Fez — fat lip.

The police came out from Dubbo and took our three kidnappers away, but not before Mrs Whittington had time to question them very carefully.

Afterwards she said, 'I don't know, Blue. They didn't say a word, but I wouldn't be surprised if those ruffians knew something about the three escaped prisoners from Sydney.'

Six Months Later ...

Tuesday, 7 November

Banjo was right. My diary came in very handy. It was taken as evidence for the upcoming trial of Veranda Head, Gorilla Dude and Gunman. It arrived in the mail today after being examined, copied and photographed, ready to be presented in court! That's nearly as good as being published, surely!

Folk out at the Bake are tough, so things returned to normal pretty quickly after 'The Big Kidnapping' ... except that Harry Wilson gave up on digging to China. Now he's building an aeroplane to fly to Greenland. Mr Cluff thought that was a great idea until Wes and Fez said they'd help him.

Sam's latest zucchini is sixty-four centimetres long and still going strong.

The new termite-free school is almost finished. It's brick and has special metal shutters over all the windows. Mr Cluff says they're to keep out the harsh sunlight, but we all know that they're part of the plan to make the school as Wes-and-Fez-proof as possible.

Miss McKenzie is living with Mrs Whittington, and is taking good care of her. I think she finds things like eating pineapple soup and finding goldfish in the bathtub a bit odd, but she's pretty happy.

Gerty's living back home again, but only because Miss McKenzie gave us a CD of Scottish bagpipe music which we blast out across the plains morning and night.

Wes and Fez are working on a new model chariot for Gunther. He's already humungous and greedier than Doris, Mildred and Gertrude all put together. He also has a very bad temper. He bit Wes so badly on the bum the other day that Mr Sweeney had to give him seven stitches. Now Wes has a scar on each buttock, which Fez is really jealous of.

The farm is looking great. The dams are full and the dust is gone, for now at least. The paddocks are as green as lime cordial. Soon the wheat will be ready for harvest and we'll be surrounded by a beautiful, golden-brown sea.

Mum hasn't cried since the rain came and she even ordered herself a new pair of jeans through the mail the other day. She hasn't done that for years.

And here's the biggy ...

It turns out that no-one around here has the money to send their kids to boarding school at the moment, after the drought and all. They're setting up extra computers at the new, termite-free school, so we can do year seven by correspondence!

Mat's livid. She can't believe she'll still be at the Bake after Christmas.

She gave me one of her withering stares and said, 'It's *so* humiliating. I'll be thirteen soon and I'll still be at a primary school. What will Gavin O'Donnell say? I swear I'll just *die*.'

The correspondence thing isn't forever though. It's just until we get through a good season, and then Mum and Dad will have the money to send me off to Bathurst with Sophie and Peter.

I'm reading *Seven Little Australians* for the fifteen millionth time. I've told Mum and Dad that if they ever try to send me to boarding school, I'll just run away and come home the first chance I get.

Dad just shook his head and said, 'Oh, well … I s'pose you could do worse.'

Mum doesn't really believe me. She thinks I'm kidding.

But I'm not.

I can survive droughts and dust storms, angry outbursts from Matilda Jane the Mature and being held hostage. I can even survive living with Wes and Fez and four mad pigs.

But I can't survive being away from home. Hillrose Poo is where I belong.

I'm just meant to have red dirt between my toes!

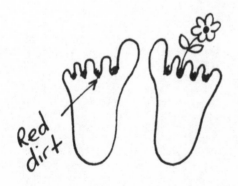

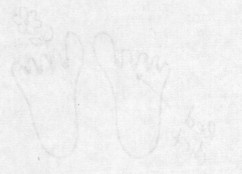

About the author

Katrina Nannestad grew up in central west New South Wales. After studying arts and education at the University of New England in Armidale, she worked as a primary school teacher. Her first teaching job was at a tiny two-teacher school in the bush. Katrina now lives near Bendigo with her husband, two sons and a pea-brained whippet.

Read Blue's next adventure ...

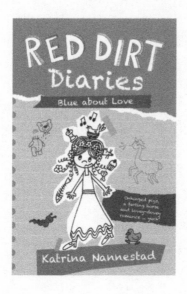

I'm going to be a bridesmaid.
Mat, Lynette and me.
Long, pink shiny dresses and flowers in our hair.
Leading Miss McKenzie down the aisle to disaster.
I think I'm going to puke ...

When Blue's favourite teacher announces she's engaged, Blue thinks she must have lost her mind. Why would Miss McKenzie want to get married? Especially to someone named James Linley Welsh-Pearson! Surely it couldn't be because she loves him — could it?

Can Blue stop the wedding in time or will Miss McKenzie leave Hardbake Plains ... forever?

Blue's adventures continue in ...

Blue Weston is on a mission!

* She's starting Hardbake Plains' first ever newspaper with Mat and Ben
* She's determined not to like her new teacher, the Colonel
* And she's trying to convince Miss McKenzie to come back from Scotland

But despite Blue's best intentions, things don't go exactly to plan ... And to make matters worse, her mum is dusting off the old boarding school uniform!

Can Blue get things back on track?

And boarding school? Her parents wouldn't dare ...